EXACTING CLAM No. 3 — Winter 2021

C000243407

CONTENTS

2	Brian Evenson	Whet
3	Thomas Walton	Unsavory Thoughts
6	Mike Silverton	The Dada Within
8	Julian Stannard	Spaghetti Alle Rossetti
13	Kevin Boniface	Cider, Milk, Sausages
15	M.J. Nicholls	Derek Meets Lord Baron Archer of Weston-Super-Mare
17	Paul Kavanagh	Hell
18	Sarah Pazur	The Shopper
22	Doug Nufer	a raven
25	Stephen Moles	Pure Meaning
26	Marvin Cohen	Cohen's Useful Directions
28	David Winner	Shrunk
32	Colin Gee	Dear John
33	Tyler C. Gore	December 26
35	John Patrick Higgins	Silvia
38	Will Alexander	Nervous Electrical Compounding
39	Andrew McKeown	O Come O Come
43	Linda Mannheim	At Liberty
45	Maureen Owen	Three Poems
47	Kurt Luchs	Choose a Star: David Ignatow and the Power of Plain Speaking
48	Kurt Luchs	For My Daughters
49	Robert Musil	Excerpts from Aphorisms (tr. Genese Grill)
51	Jake Goldsmith	On CF and Possibility
53	R.S. Mengert	Two Poems
55	LJ Pemberton	Triangles Are Not Circles
58	Jesse Salvo	Safe Seat
61	Matthew Tomkinson	Livn Inthwrld
63	Ben Pester	square / recess / moon
69	Casmilus	Polymorphous Polyester: Isabel Waidner's Sterling Karat Gold
70	Jesi Buell	Strange Bloodlines: Marcus Pactor's Begat Who Begat Who Begat
71	M.J. Nicholls	Reviews in Brief
74	Kurt Luchs	Whitney Collins' Big Bad
75	Colin James	A Vampire's Neologisms
77	John Oliver Hodges	White Roses
79	Paul John Adams	Windows into Mike Kleine's Universe
83	A. Salcedo	Poem V, from The Hydrogen Mafia (tr. Daniel Beauregard)
84	Chris Sumberg	Wednesday Morning, Rain

Front cover: "Shall I Be Mother?" by John Patrick Higgins
Inside cover illustrations by Kathleen Nicholls
Interior drawings by John Patrick Higgins & Gutenberg Project
© 2021 Sagging Meniscus Press
All Rights Reserved
ISBN: 978-1-952386-30-5
Exacting Clam is a quarterly publication from Sagging Meniscus.

Senior Editors: Aaron Anstett, Jesi Bender, Jeff Chon, Elizabeth Cooperman, Tyler C. Gore, Charles Holdefer, Kurt Luchs, M.J. Nicholls, Doug Nufer, Thomas Walton
Executive Editor: Guillermo Stitch <guillermostitch@saggingmeniscus.com>
Publisher: Jacob Smullyan <smulloni@saggingmeniscus.com>
exactingclam.com

Brian Evenson

Whet

I am not going to suggest to you that a butcher knife is better than a boning knife. Even a paring knife can be formidable in the right hands. Choose your knife based on your own familiarity with that variety of knife and your sense of the corpulence of your victim (if you know—if you have simply been passing through backyards checking for unlocked doors and unsecured sliders, you may not). No, my sole advice is that you acquire your knife at the house in which it will be used.

You may object that the problem with getting a knife at the house in which it will be used is you can never tell how people are at sharpening them. You get a dull one and it slips or turns instead of slicing through and, there, you've cut yourself, left a bit of yourself at the scene. Before you know it, they've got a bead on you.

But you can't bring a knife from home either. That's no good once they show up at your house and realize that you're a knife short of a block. Or once they discover that, despite your precautions, despite all the scrubbing, there is still a daub of blood between the tang and the scales of the knife you sentimentally kept.

And you can't be the kind of person who just goes around buying knives willy-nilly. That gets noticed too.

No, you have to be prepared to make the most of whatever is at hand. Bring a whetstone with you and then, once you choose a knife from their block or from their drawer, take a few minutes to sharpen it. If you practice at home, you'll soon be able to sharpen a knife by feel, in the dark. It becomes, so I have found, a meditative practice that can center you marvelously, the whsk-whsking of the blade over stone making you acutely aware of your connection to everything that surrounds you, including the person or persons you are about to kill.

It is difficult to enter a properly meditative state if your intended is tied up, hard to focus when someone is screaming, albeit muffledly, into a gag. Better to take the risk that nobody in the house will awaken to hear the gentle sound of stone whetting steel. And if they do, or, if, say, an inhabitant of the household comes downstairs in search of a glass of milk, well, at very least the knife is sharper than it was a few moments before. And if it is still not sharp enough, if you nevertheless cut yourself and leave a trace, nobody is perfect. If necessary, once your work with the knife is done, you can always burn the house to the ground.

Thomas Walton

Unsavory Thoughts

Disparate Thoughts Lacking Much Moon

Where in this universe can I find a way out of its laws? Isn't that what we all want? Or should I jump in with transcendent pragmatism to contemplate my inevitable demise: the fact I no longer jump, run fast, or touch my toes without groaning. Maybe if I dig a hole in the backyard and crawl in it, and pull the soil back over me, maybe that's where transcendence is hiding?

The Etruscans, perhaps, knew best to decorate their tombs with lovely things. No mere hole for them! But a room brilliant with frescos of seascapes and gardens. All their most cherished possessions with them: amphoras of wine, oil, feasts laid out around them, friends even, and dogs and lovers.

The trick, I guess, is to get to your tomb before you wind up in somebody else's . . . whether as a dog, a lover, or both.

I suppose you can no longer write about the moon. There are now so many taboos. We live in an age of myriad taboos. There are times it seems nothing can be said without offending someone. Even that sentiment will come across as offensive. It's gotten so bad, so exhaustive all this endless correcting, that you wind up throwing up your hands and just saying whatever you want, realizing no matter how careful you are, someone somehow will take offense.

But don't worry, I won't say a thing about the moon.

The older you get, the more exotic young people become. What on earth are they doing? Are they so captive in their own bodies that they've lost their minds? I suppose so. There's probably nothing to be done. They will age, and see their folly, and new ones will replace them.

But where are they going driven by "that place where procreation flares . . ."? Flares is certainly the right word. A mere flash, a flicker or fast second here, a whole life—to say nothing of the desire to multiply. Is it "go forth and multiply" or "sit down and shut up"? At some point the latter surely comes knocking on the door of the former.

But who's to say which of us should be the ones to forgo regeneration? We all demand the right to contribute to the decadent overpopulation of our colony. Show me any human and I will show you a colonist. Show me any animal at all, any plant for that matter. It is the nature of nature to end in what's unnatural.

And yet, that's the thing with nature: it can hold all things. It's as hungry and as flexible as the English language, so that even the unnatural becomes subsumed as something natural after all.

No, I'm afraid the youth will not help out with this one. Again. We're on our own, meaning, we'll never find a place to be alone.

Perfect Readers

I don't like to tell people what I'm reading. It seems pretentious. I don't really like to talk about books at all. At least not with most people. Certainly not with other writers! The best people to talk about books with are people who don't write, who only read.

Of course, there are people who only read to "better themselves." I don't like those people. How could I? They ask you what you're reading in the same way they might ask you what your politics are. Those people only read the books in fashion. And by "in fashion" I mean in political fashion. It's disgusting.

Of course, I talk about books with my wife. She is a writer, but she's also my wife (that's two strikes against her). We have to talk about books, as, like most married people, we are constantly trying to find things to talk about.

And sometimes, because we live together, one of us will just start talking and the other one will overhear, and they will sometimes be talking about books. We are lucky in that we mostly read different things. But not always. Sometimes we read the same things . . . on purpose! This can be, at its best, interesting. At its worst we argue for days about whether the language of Choderlos de Laclos is too florid, the sentimentality of Maggie Nelson is too cloying, or if the bits about Jesus in Pascal should be cut out altogether. The arguments become memes, and inevitably personal. And because we are both writers, we insult not only the other's intelligence, but by extension their writing as well. Now, insulting a writer's intelligence is not that big of a deal. They don't really care. But if you insult their writing they will be absolutely devastated and sulk for weeks!

The only literary thing my wife and I have ever agreed on is that Dostoevsky's Svidrigalov is the most perfect villain (outside of Shakespeare) in all of literature.

My friend Tyler, I think, is the perfect reader. First of all, he doesn't write. Secondly, he is endlessly patient. He's read William Gass's fiction for godssakes! He doesn't seem to form snap judgements or let his ego intercede in the story. He just watches it happen. It's very passive but that might be the best way to read: to surrender completely to the writer. After all, a book is not a conversation, it's an argument, a proposition. You can only have conversations *about* a book, not with it. In fact, I think that's why a lot of writers write in the first place. We can say whatever we want without anyone talking back to us. By the time a reader does talk back, we've already stopped talking and moved on to something else, "oh, yeah, whatever, I'm not really interested in that anymore . . ."

The more I think about it, the more I'm convinced that the best way to read a book is to just let it happen to you. Like watching a horror movie, or therapy. You have to just let it happen or it doesn't work . . . The time for objection comes when the text is done, which I suppose in this instance would be . . . now.

No Shoes Are Better Than Four

I never liked clothes. I wear them of course, but I would be happy not to. Or to wear the bare minimum (bare being the operative word). I could live where it's warm, and wear only swimmers, at most a loose shirt or linen slacks at night. Never socks. I hate socks. Socks feel like little straitjackets for your feet. The worst part of my day is putting on socks, and I leave it till the last possible minute, and take them off as soon as I can. Sometimes I take them off on my way home from work. I drive barefoot.

The times I've lived where it's warm have been the most healthy and contented days of my life. Even Taiwan, where the air is full of dust and lead and carbon monoxide, the fact that socks were not necessary made up for the sinus infections, the thick yellow mucus, the burning eyes and the potential for lung cancer.

In Mexico, too, socks are unnecessary. What's the point? Sure, people get dressed up there (as they do in Taiwan) but there's no need to. Why? Just sit on the *terraza* and listen to the parrots, the mariachi, or the men yelling "*elote!*" in the street.

I went a whole year without wearing socks in Australia. It was delightful. I nearly floated away. Socks are a burden, an anchor. They are the chain that ties Prometheus to the stone so the vultures can pick out his eyes. What fool invented them? What pretentious, Edwardian shithead said "Oh, these will adorn the area above the shoe and beneath the hem."

A sock is a shoe, etymologically speaking, and therefore unnecessary. What fool would wear two pairs of shoes? From Old English, *socc*, "a kind of light shoe," derived from Greek, *sukkhos*, "a Phrygian shoe." Phrygia is where Turkey is now. It is of course a desert country on the Mediterranean: a place where you don't need socks! I don't blame the Phrygians for wearing shoes, especially "light shoes," but what dumbass, from what country, decided "these shoes work better if you wear another shoe on top of them?"

On Death and Failure

I admit I think of death as kind of a failure. A tragedy, to be sure, but also a failure. I'm just being honest.

The geranium in the balcony box, for instance. It came back again this spring, and is blooming now in May. The verbena, though, didn't make it. It failed to. I planted them both at the same time, in the same way, under the same circumstances.

I saw a rat that had been run over by a car. It had been there for some time, as it was flat against the pavement. All of its guts squeezed out through its mouth and ass, the hole in its side where it burst like a balloon. Many cars had run over it. I was riding my bike, and I saw it, and I took a picture of it with my phone. To have as a kind of memento mori.

I'm not trying to be insensitive. None of us have much control, ultimately. But it does seem to be a failure of certain species that they cannot achieve longevity. Some insects have only minutes on this earth, a day at most. While a tree might live a thousand years. That tree, to me, is a great success.

When I say certain species, I mean individuals of certain species, of course (see rat above).

A moth who lives a few moments longer is as much of a success as a tree that makes it a few decades more.

And what is *our* problem! Most of us, if we're lucky, make it seventy or eighty years. That's it! Randomly flipping through the dictionary, I see that Pat Nixon lived to be eighty-one. Richard Nixon also eighty-one. George Mason (American Revolutionary) died at sixty-seven. Eleanor Roosevelt was ninety. Even Socrates lived to be seventy-one. It seems to me we've failed if we haven't been able to improve our life expectancy more than a few years on someone who lived over 2,300 years ago. That, surely, is a failure.

But maybe those moths, a few minutes old, have always lived to be only a few minutes old. Maybe we're stuck, fixed in the wax of our biological limitations. And all we can do (again, if we're lucky) is fill out the full potential of our measly seventy or eighty years. Bask in the sun that long, before the lights go out, again, forever.

Mike Silverton

The Dada Within

From *Anvil on a Shoestring*
(Sagging Meniscus, 2022)

We are fortunate as a society that certain endeavors require certification. Should I one day awaken convinced I've an aptitude for reconstructive dental surgery, pediatric oncology, gastroenterology, ophthalmology, veterinary medicine or, sidewise, electrical engineering, it would not be unreasonable to haul me away in a strait jacket. At the very least you'd best decline my offer to rewire your home. Or neuter your kitten.

However, "It's a free country" obtains in practices less available to prosecutorial scrutiny. Charlatans come fast to mind, especially in the God dodge. To explore deeper here would plunge me into a simmering rage, nor do I propose to impose on the reader's patience.

Obviously, given our context, we're about the arts. Creativity. Dare we say it, sublimity. The transcendental. From certain angles and in a certain light, the divine. The Good Lord willin' and the crapper don't back up, when all goes flawlessly, unreasonably—nay, miraculously—well, something interesting might happen. While it's true that art schools and writing workshops exist, with proofs of attendance moreover, individuals can with a clear conscience declare themselves artists or writers, or maybe both in the same carcass, on the strength of a say-so.

"I'm a writer."

"Have you published anything?"

"Not yet."

Therefore and so forth and by my green candle to state one's theme, I am in the great tradition of soi-disantitude a full-feathered Dada innocent of validation beyond the skin I occupy. Nihil obstat. Devil take the hindmost. Damn the torpedoes but be mindful of the reef.

To which forebears is one especially beholden? To Marcel Duchamp, certainly. His lifelong insouciance remains a standard to emulate, not to neglect the readymade, Art's tectonic shift. In a broader sense, to Alfred Jarry and his assault on propriety. I stand in particular admiration of his gift to humankind, 'pataphysics, an as yet immeasurable leap beyond metaphysics. Yet am I reluctant to acquire membership in the Collège de Same Name inasmuch as this requires application and (I'm guessing) a registration fee. From a respectful distance I continue to admire 'pataphysics's embrace of imaginary solutions, no less the impertinent apostrophe. Assigning to the already large Cosmos an exponential expansion, more likely infinite, introduces freedoms as gratifying as good afternoon sex.

We won't complicate the discussion with Thespis's offspring. Further, I'll endeavor to keep autobiography to a barely audible mumble, notwithstanding some good stuff, e.g., my having deflowered Shirley Temple. For another time. *The Dada Within* is a topic—to be hoped—of general interest and application. Indeed, but what do you mean by Dada, granddad?

Can we agree to call it a free-wheeling, sometimes destabilizing state of mind?

To begin, my identification with Dada flounders in anachronism. Call it twilit senescence. Geriatric willfulness. I align with the originals in the Cabaret Voltaire despite having little in common, least of all one's wardrobe. Europe, at the height of a rather fastidious civilization, descended into a war the duration and ferocity of which took all by surprise. The machine gun

layed a prominent role. (I digress: given the run
n guns and the price of ammunition, when avail-
ble—blame the pandemic and the right wing's
ribal drift—shooting a fully automatic weapon at a
ange is a luxury just south of Patek Philippe. I
ught to have mentioned earlier that one's Jarry
dmiration also looks to sidearms. The reader may
now of this anecdote. Jarry was shooting his re-
olver in a backyard. A neighbor complained that
his reckless behavior endangered her son. Should
hat possibility become a reality,
arry offered to help the lady
make another.)

Anger, disillusion, cyni-
ism, la vie bohème's per-
istent undertow, all (as
he narrative has it) ex-
plain why Dada
popped up at its
moment in his-
ory. At a far
emove from
he War to
ind All Wars
t pleases this
antasist to
hink that ab-
surdity's culti-
vation and matu-
ation better describe
Dada's precious bodily flu-
ds as and where they nowa-
days flow.

Does a sharply drawn line between Dada and
Surrealism exist? Hardly. Or maybe. Or no. Or yes.
A good deal of Surrealist art seems to me Dada in
spirit. Max Ernst's painting of the Virgin Mother
spanking a young Jesus's bare ass, with Surrealism's heavy hitters looking on through a window is
pure Dada. Freud's subconscious plays no role in
this psychodrama. René Magritte's work is Surrealist in its dream-like aspect and Dada in its

drollery. This can be said: Surrealism in its French
heyday was authoritarian. Andy Breton ran a tight
ship. More than a few heretics walked the plank.
The Dadas were anarchic. A favorite Dada object,
Man Ray's *Gift*, is an upright clothing iron, its plate
lined down the center with a row of spikes (glued
nails, actually). It was my great good luck to find a
miniature wooden ironing board of the same period, intended, I believe, for shirt sleeves, to
which, in homage, I glued a line of nails and hung
on a wall—a footnote to a brilliant absurdity.

As a writer, I identify with participants in a
movement I might well have regarded with
suspicion and, who knows, disdain were I a
contemporary in fact rather than tepid
spirit. As a good, law-abiding bour-
geois, this anachronistic impulse
began a ton of years ago and
continues with
chance opera-
tions—the
gathering of
alphabetical shrapnel I
fashion over stretches of time into
images, thoughts and asso-
ciations that,
when all goes
well, engage and
perhaps even startle
and amuse. I welcome
beauty to remain in the be-
holder's eye. Nor am I much con-
cerned with the participation of my subconscious
or unconscious. They're on their own. Look, if the
superficial dazzles, depth need not apply. Think of
spectral insects skimming across a still pond, lightly
disturbing the water's surface. In bright sunlight.
With frogs. Lily pads even.

Spaghetti alle Rossetti

Radio Requests

I lost last year my wife of fifty years, sweet Mavis.
Would you, could you play some Miles Davis?

My partner's gotten Alzheimer's.
The days have shrunk.
Spread some joy with Thelonious Monk.

I lost my father, the days are darker.
Could you play some Charlie Parker?

I kicked my addiction to cocaine.
If you could play anything by John Coltrane
I'd open another bottle of champagne.

A kumquat for a quintet.
                    A jazz band in a dream land!

I recently switched gender. I call myself Cherry.
I'd dance across the room if you played Chuck Berry.

Last year was a train wreck.
Time, surely, for Dave Brubeck.

The days are grey, the sky is gloopy.
Energise us with Fela Kuti.

Last year my husband was so unkind
I ran away.
Could you play something by Billie Holiday?

I popped the question to my girlfriend Jean.
A thumbs up!
We're gagging for some Bunky Green.

My auntie's knitting Kashmiri shawls.
A sudden blast of Biggie Smalls?

After thirty years of marriage
my wife threw in the towel—

(leaping off a bridge)—
Oh Daisy! Daisy! Daisy!
She was always partial to Count Basie.

Shall we, shan't we, should we, let's.
Give us something by Stan Getz.

This year I gave birth to Jerome.
Almost anything please by Nina Simone!

It was our first wedding anniversary last year
(I don't normally tell people this,
I met my husband at Walmart . . .)
We lowered the blinds,
a tip-top afternoon with Django Reinhart.
Would you? Could you? Should you?

So I grabbed it online and paid the acquisition fee!
Bring on the trumpets, Dizzy Gillespie.

I recently qualified as a Level Two Undertaker.
Please play My Funny Valentine by Chet Baker.

We lost dear Max on Boxing Day.
Our loving selfless Dachshund dog.
Could we hear the voice of Karin Krog?

My dentist went completely mad
and pulled out all my teeth.
I now make a weird sucking noise
which goes quite well with 'Tootie' Heath.

Last year I had a stroke.
I would like to listen to some Elmo Hope.

Last year another breakdown, I was sent away . . .
Reel me back with Sydney Bechet.

A kumquat for a quintet.
                A jazz band in a dream land!

Last month I gave up and laid down
for the last time my weary head.
Could you play The Grateful Dead?

Keep Two metres Apart, Save Lives, It Said

at the entrance to the graveyard.
Dear dead people you should relax,
turn a blind eye, two blind eyes
if you prefer. I would advise you
to shake your bones and disinter.

Lean over to a corpse

in ectoplasmic ecstasy.

Now that you are dead you're safe!

Dear safe dead people
a large man in white gloves is standing
in the middle of the graveyard,
singing *Nessun Dorma! Nessun Dorma!*

He's scattering rose petals here and there.

Dear dead people,
I would urge the letting down of your hair.

Consider that pre-Raphaelite beauty
whose fiery curls blossomed and bloomed
filling the coffin after death.

The worms agog—

(An endless plate of perfectly cooked
and freshly seasoned Spaghetti Alle Rossetti.)

The dead, the un-dead, the half-dead—
The determinedly-doggedly dead—
The occasional—Hardyesque—dog head—

Huggermugger.

And when I walk home late
through the graveyard
I will not complain
if an arm reaches out
and grabs me by the leg.

Duck Corner

I'll meet you at Duck Corner.

                            I'll be riding Gauloises
my newly acquired horse.

He used to clop along
Boulevard Saint-Michel
singing *Le Monde Entier Fait Boum!*

with Simone de Beauvoir
and Jean-Paul Sartre.

Of course—

Now it's Duck Corner . . .

In fact the only person who isn't there
is you!

I like it when you're late.
Even better when you're dead—

So déjà vu.
I should be stricken by remorse.

If my mouth could open wider
I'd smoke the entire horse.

Have you noticed
our meetings at Duck Corner never work out?

The hooves of the horse are hoofing.
It's so wretchedly déjà vu.

Have you read *The Magnificent Smoking Horse*
by Albert Camus?

Jamaica Road

I walked down Jamaica Road in terrible rain.
Natalia and Jenny and Jack washed away . . . .
An old lady pulled me to my feet
linking arms, helping me up and on—
and helping herself to my wallet.
What disappointment when she opens it.

After much Weialala leia Wallala leialala
I fetched up in Charles' sitting room
in Shepherd's Bush—Oh green so green and wet
so wet is Shepherd's Bush this rain-soaked night
and many flights of stairs above me.

One time I slept at the top, miles away—
I was a midshipman in the crow's nest,
watching Napoleon
making his way down the Uxbridge Road
like a crab thermidor.

I was cat sitting.
I could hear the cats down in the kitchen murmuring
Feed us! Feed us!

The bedraggled having walked down Jamaica Road me
is reading *Notes Without A Text*
with Harold on my shoulder
(he's quite forgiven me . . .)

Charles is rewriting *The Brothers Karamazov*
upstairs somewhere
with a typewriter—clackety-clack.
He's making such a racket.

He's taking out the padding
and focusing on the good bits
making sure each character has only one name
which they stick to, or at least try to—

What a slim publication it's going to be.

A couple's making out on the stoop.
Couldn't you use another stoop? I say.
We like this one.
But it's raining.
We like doing it in the rain.
You have a problem with that?

Well yes, well no, oh   oh

Kevin Boniface

Cider, Milk, Sausages

6.00am: There's no daylight at this time of the morning but my neighbour's security lights compensate for that. At the back of the house, music leaks from the garage where the radio is left to play all night to dissuade would-be intruders.

A car drifts by with searchlight headlights. A robin is singing down by the railway line.

On, past the stone owl, fox and eagle arranged on the hardstanding under the washing line which sags under the weight of half-a-dozen wet t-shirts.

Into the park where a heron flies over the SpongeBob SquarePants merry-go-round and the ducks pad listlessly around the pond. A small bag of dog shit has been left on the stone lip of the temperance fountain.

7.00am: From the first-floor window of the delivery office I can see the church gardens are almost deserted. One man in a black hooded top sits alone on a bench in the lee of the church tower. I watch as he gets to his feet and performs an intricate dance routine while clutching a large blue Co-op bag in his left hand. When two other men enter the gardens, cutting through to the bus stop, he abruptly sits back down.

8.00am: At the bus stop the pensioners are in conversation. "When the weather's like this you wouldn't want to go abroad anyway, would you?"

In the church gardens the drunks are in conversation. "What are you fucking having a fucking go at me for? What's he having a fucking go at me for?"

Inside the delivery office, my colleagues are in conversation. "We didn't just win it, we bossed them. We bossed them off the park".

On the expensive new estate, a woman is in conversation with her dog walker. "I'm going to have to buy a new wet suit, I can't get into the one I bought last year. Tim's going to have to get one as well, his is two years old!"

9.00am Ducks again! And buddhas and fuchsias and fairies and gnomes and robins and cats with binoculars and fuchsias and hedgehogs and phlox and crocosmia and verbena and holly and some late alstroemeria and ducks and fuchsias and a mole wearing glasses climbing out of a plant pot.

"Morning!" I say to the builders in the driveway of the house they are working on. They both look up briefly but don't reply.

10.00am: At the big new house in the picturesque village on the moor I knock on the imposing front door. A school mate I've not seen for thirty-five years appears at the window. He doesn't recognise me. I hold up a parcel and he holds up two fingers. "Two seconds!" he says before revising his estimate, "One second". He then disappears for a total of thirty-three seconds before returning with the key to the door.

At the house with the breathtaking views, I ask if anybody recognises the name on the handwritten letter from Denmark with no number on the address. The woman who rarely smiles says she doesn't. "Ask them at 28" she says, "They're really nosey. If anyone knows, they will."

The horse in the field at the side of the track down to Moor End Farm always stares at the van as I pass. It seems surprised. Every day it's as though it's just there looking over its wall and it sees me in a bright red Peugeot Partner, and it thinks *What the fuck is that?*

11.00am: The man in the shorts, neon trainers and mirror sunglasses is dragging two English bulldogs along the tow path. He calls one of them Rogue and the other 'You fucking spaz'.

"D'you drink beer, lad?" asks the man in his 60s who is shovelling hardcore into the potholes of the muddy forecourt of the brewery. "Yes" I say. "Well, we're having a do on Saturday. Get yourself down here and bring plenty of money." "I'll be working" I explain. The man turns his attention to the woman in the pink anorak who is passing with her dog. He leans on his shovel, "Here's a lovely lady for equality!" He shouts. "Equality?" says the woman, looking confused. "Yes" says the brewery man, "Equality for us men". The woman rolls her eyes and continues on her way.

The woman who is working out to a loud high-energy soundtrack doesn't hear me when I knock at her door, so I leave her parcel with her neighbour, the man with the dinner down his shirt whose doorbell sounds like a chaffinch.

The Iceland delivery truck is parked up in an isolated spot on a country lane in the woods while the driver uses it for cover. He's pissing into the mother-die on the verge, he has his cock in one hand and a cigarette in the other.

1.00pm: It's raining beech nuts at Wood-field House. They're bouncing off the parked cars, the big council wheelie bins, the mail-boxes, the stone gateposts and my head. The treetops are alive with squirrels.

On the track down to the farm I pass the bloody remains of a collard dove left on the verge by a sparrowhawk. A few yards further down, a dead rabbit, eyes pecked out by the crows, lies splayed under a five-bar gate.

2.00pm: "Right!" says the man adjusting his face mask and bending for a basket at the entrance to the Co-op, "Cider, milk, sausages".

3.00pm: I'm having no luck trying to shoo an enormous fly out of the window and the neighbours who live in the house where the man who looked like Charles Bukowski used to live are arguing in the street. They are all wearing their 'Sunday best' and the man in his thirties whose shirt is untucked is shouting "I've fucking apologised! Why won't you fucking accept my fucking apology?" He turns to the woman who is retrieving her handbag from a small red Kia Picanto. "This is my day, stop making me out to be the cunt!" A hearse arrives with the word DAD spelled out in chrysanthemums displayed against the side of the coffin. It pulls up in front of the Picanto and the man tucks in his shirt and puts out his cigarette. I trick the fly out of the window but another one comes in before I have time to shut it again.

11.00pm: I'm walking home and I'm quite drunk. I think the man on the mountain bike might be drunk too because he rides into a parked car and ends up on his back in the road. He gets to his feet, wrestles the bike upright and struggles back into the saddle. He spins the peddles wildly but the bike goes nowhere, the chain has come off. He curses. "Hey, Mate!" He shouts as I pass "Do you know if there's a hairdresser or a barbers open round here?" "You'll be lucky at this time" I say. He wanders off pushing the bike and cursing loudly.

DEPT. OF GRAVE FROTTAGE

At last, my name in print! —aspiring writer's epitaph

Even if there is not life after death, there is sex after pizza.

On Gissing's Edwin

He tried,
then he died.

M.J. Nicholls

Derek Meets Lord Baron Archer of Weston-Super-Mare

From *The Fall & Fall of Derek Haffman*
(Sagging Meniscus, Nov. 2022)

Derek's stomach said: "Yes, I can see. I can see Camilla, that ballad of middle-aged elegance, that corrido of poise and pertness, that torch song of above-average intelligence and wit, towering over Millie like a cougar teasing a wounded beaver. Yes, I can see. I can see Archer manspreading on that chair in a state of priapic anticipation at the lawsuit about to impend in our face like a runaway camion burning down Filbert Street, San Fran. But I couldn't care less. I am a stomach, my friend. As a stomach, I seek nutritional satisfaction. I have one simple demand. I want two rashers of bacon and a black pudding. Please fulfil this need immediately and exempt me from any oncoming emotional turmoil."

Derek's bladder said: "Yes, I can sense. I can sense the awkward stalemate in the room. No one willing to unspool the tickertape of shrieking hell-ack running in their heads into a neat line of 're-alistic' dialogue. I can sense the heart-burning re-riminations and the anthrax-strength venom soon to emerge from the mouths of those present named Camilla. I can sense the bubbles of super-ilious phlegm soon to flow from the mouths of those present named Jeffrey. But I couldn't care less. I am a bladder, my friend. As a bladder, I seek the mere release of the liquids and uric acid from any person through your little person. Please fulfil this need immediately and exempt me from any unpleasant self-soiling."

"Well, I suppose I better speak, if no one else will," Camilla spoke as no one else would. Her intimidatingness in a floral blouse and flowing purple skirt was as strong as her intimidatingness in a business shirt and skirt of pencil. Derek's stomach and bladder had been overruled. His heart was campaigning hard for a cardiac episode, pumping at the speeds of a solar probe late for a bus. "OK," he heard himself burp.

"It's all right," Archer said, springing from the chair with the flair of a viper in £300 flipflops. "I will recommence comms. Now, Derek. We need to have a little parley, chez vou. I appreciate our presence here, as you bask like an ITV4 Tristan and Isolde in the Spanish sunshine, is unexpected. Rather like a sudden onslaught of midges in a forest clearing, as I wrote rather poetically in one of the novels."

Camilla kept her place at the TV stand hovering over a melting Millie, unseated from reality on the bed's edge in her sweaty pants.

"Hi, I'm the wife," she said, no hand offered. Millie reflexed a hand upwards, hanging that hand in the air in wait for a polite reciprocal to leap palm-to-palm in a show of sisterly mercy and, seeing no such hand offered and sensing the implied snub, rerouted her hand back to tuck in her pre-tucked hair. "I'm the previous residence of Dezza's penis. I see he has swapped a five-bedroom Georgian townhouse for an outdoor privy." Millie was too embarrassed at the obvious hand rerouting failure to note the ouch. She had fallen into an emotional sump, all prior punk sunken neath the wither of a together woman.

"It came to pass, Derek, that I was sipping a latte in the VIP lounge, waiting for the boarding call, when I observed your Romanesque betrothed. I was reading proofs of the next novel—no other prose stimulates me like mine—when I observed her charming shanks nestled within the porous runnels of a skirt. She, too, was consuming a latte, that tremendous loin-stirring beverage brewed from the finest Hereford cow titties and the most flavoursome beans from the kaffirs. I approached her to remark on the coincidence of our lattes and remind her that I am Jeffrey Archer—yes, that one from the Monica Coghlan affair and the accidentally stolen Canadian suits—and to enquire whether her legs had won the Turner Prize. She informed me that she was making an impromptu trip to see her husband who had eloped with a mistress, and that her husband was Derek Haffman MSP, meaning he played politics in the sandpit Westminster permitted the Scotch to build for themselves. I made a whooping sound. I whooped! The others in the VIP lounge were treated to the rare spectacle of me, that Jeffrey Archer, that one from the umpteen failed London mayoral attempts, from the short period in chokey, making a whoop! You can complete the rest, Derek. I told her I was on the hunt for a prime piece of libel meat."

The length of Archer's prattle was the exact time needed for a thought to send a message to Derek's mouth and for his mouth to send a message to his brain asking for permission from his brain to send approval to his mouth.

"Look, Lord Archer—"

"Now, now! I haven't finished. I always used to tell Cecil Parkinson, my conversation has natural rhythms, Parkie. Sometimes I pause to allow the wingèd wasp of a notion to buzz around the perimeter of my ponderance and permit entrance to the auricle of sapience. Sometimes I leave time for the absorption of a classic Archer ponderance into the room's gullet. My thoughts are large aspirins, fizzling themselves into people's brains with a salving wisdom, clearing the rot from their thinking so that clear-headed sense propels them forward to admitting I am right. Let me explain. I have a crack team of Libel Lugworms. I send these Lugworms into the world to see what anti-Archer libel they can dredge up from the sludge of the ar-

chives, then I reel in their catch to inspect wha Archerish anguish I might have caused to meri the slander. In most cases, the libel is unworkable But I never miss the chance."

"You've come to sue me?" Derek asked. Listen ing to the wretched man's obscene self-confidenc as the sentences flowed from his wrinkle-carve and winkie-pink head into the shredder of his ear forced Derek to shift his stance from spooke okapi to sarcastic lemur.

"Kane and Abel! You're quite the impatien penitent, Deccadent. I'm here to offer what I lik to call frienemesistance. It's a mouthful, I agree Let's break it down. It's a portmanteau word com bining the nouns 'friend', 'nemesis', and 'assis tance'. You see, I come as a frienemesis, meanin; neither friend nor nemesis and friend and neme sis. To clarify, I come to offer the sort of assistanc to one who is neither friend nor nemesis who i. also a friend and a nemesis. You might think thes contradictions. Not in the world of Jeffrey, me lad In my world, a man is always a frienemesis, some one on whom you can rely or hatchet in the ster num when the occasion arises. This is the world o the élites, Derek. There are no friends or nemese: where I prowl. Friends are merely people in a tem porary waiting list for supreme annihilation at the sweetest possible moment. This is the world at the highest level of politics, success, wealth, and fame It's an absolute delirium of human relations up here."

"Much as I'm finding this lexical dawdle an exquisite earfuck, can we speed up, please?" Camilla asked.

She crossed her arms in that classic, time-tested show of impatience.

"Of course, Camilla. Now, permit me to limn the nature of our relations, Derek, through frienemesistance. We will proceed as friends (in the sense of friends in the rubric of frienemeses) until such a time when we must proceed as neme-

16

es (in the sense of frienemeses), and so on. Do not mistake me, Hasselhaff. This relationship is a pendulum. I am on hugging terms with men whose insides I have vacuumed out, their airless husks hung on the washing line for my own glory. I am on hugging terms with men who have pistol-whipped me into twelve irreversible comas. Because we know the rules. There are no friends or nemeses. There are people to exploit at the exact moment it becomes advantageous. This is the relationship I intend to pursue with yourself, Derek. Now, I shall repair to the nearest marisquería for some of the Mediterranean's finest scallops while your wife conducts herself."

She uncrossed her arms in that classic, time-tested show of exasperation at having to wait for a man to shut up.

"Thank you, Jeffrey."

Paul Kavanagh

Hell

I leave the house and there they are lingering apple dappled Eve & Adam blood drenched Heloise & Abelard tommygun peppered Clyde & Bonnie. Recto she lissom short sitting on the wall. Verso he hirsute and burly married to the wall. I'm in the gutter in the canal in the culvert caught between recto and verso like a louse between thumb and forefinger like a fly between wall and newspaper like a sausage between fork and knife. Laughable the wall soon to be a pile of red bricks beautiful red bricks missiles for the riots to come. I am damned double damned cursed and plagued triple damned. Dante whispering Virgil pointing. Should I wave. Do not provoke them. I provoke them. It's going to be a lovely day he threatens. A hot day she condemns. I close the gate she jumps to her feet he parts company with the wall. They are full to bursting with japes larks bon mots windups. Asp bitten Cleopatra & Tony redheadabhorrers Helen & Paris. Brick through a window. I hurry like a bee in the bum like a duck in the dick like a hornet in the hole. They must be a couple have to be a couple maybe not they are always together though but they seem detached almost at war with each other bruised and battered Judy & Punch. We are not a threesome a trinity a triptych three Popes. Primo she pokes. Secondo he prods. Tertius walks. They follow. Her breathing uneven and rank and he burps and belches. I hurry. These diaphanous paronomasias plague me. They keep up. I bob my head. They bob. Ring around nine times and stop at Malebolge's off-license for spirits. We stop and drink. They whistle when I whistle we cough we swear we fart we spit we walk under ladders we seek out the one magpie kick the black cat crack mirrors seek out the evil eye and our shadows mix our airs even our thoughts. We are not a threesome. We'll show him hell she says. Yes we will he says. Look he's pissed in his trousers she says. Look he's shite in his trousers he says. He's a drug fiend she says. He's a pervert he says. Walks like he's been on a horse for a year she says. Walks like a duck he says. Walks like he needs a hammering she says. Walks like he has a redhot poker shoved up his anus he says. Should I turn. Should I confront them. Should I offer to fight him. 1. The fist. 2. The broken nose. 3. The gaps in his diseased teeth. 4. The scar over his left eye. 5. The tattoos. 6. The height. 7. The weight. 8. Her killer look. 9. Her cruel mouth. 10. Her ferret eyes. 11. Her high heels. I rub my face in desperation. Sigh. They rub. They sigh. We all sigh. I start to run they run we run pick up the pace fast and furious almost flying unquestionably sweating I smell them they smell me up lanes down roads across highways over fields through mudbaths cleaving though shitheaps onto the wasteland. I stop. Lucrezia Borgia shrugs Niccolò di Bernardo dei Machiavelli rubs his cock. Here frogs croak and lizards bite and snakes prowl a mosaic composed of the most violent acts conceivable a tapestry where the lion is attacking the Madonna where the rabbits and lambs are overwhelming the unicorn and removing the unicorn's horn with broken bottles and smashed pint glasses. Bacchus We could do it on that mattress before us Medusa We could Tityus Torture me some more. Hell is other people somebody said Kafka Camus Beckett me. I continue. They continue. We continue. A. Aroma of ass. B. Boils upon bums. C. Cleave of clunge. D. Dirt of dong. E. Earth of refrigerators televisions microwaves ovens prams beds cars. F. Fuckable the fucks. G. Gobble thy goolies. H House of hornets. I. Inside by inward. J. Jumping the jesters. K. Kicking the kitty. L. Light for lighthouse. M Mums the mumble. N. Naked to knackered. O Ovidize the oval. P. Pock the poker. Q. Queynte my Oh Now I know why Dante Alighieri tortured Francesca & Paolo. I admit it it's true I married them glued them stuck them together sexed them demanded a performance of them told them to sing and dance created them gave birth to them but how I did it is another tale all together and as you know or don't know a tale is made up with a myriad of other tales.

SaraH Pazur

THe SHoppeR

I roll over and check the text: Steve C just started shopping—we'll let you know if any item replacements need your approval.

Ugh, a male shopper. Now I'm going to have to be tied to this phone the whole time.

I am hungover. The sort of hangover that is the difference between two and three bottles of wine. Two, general malaise. Three, headache and cottonmouth. I check the time: 9:18. I immediately regret placing the order.

Steve C, your Instacart Shopper: The store does not have the requested product, Simple Truth Organic Basil

Btw my name is Steve if you need anything I'm here to help <smiley face emoji>

Hi Steve! Thanks

Hi No problem <smiley face emoji>

I'm already annoyed they don't have basil. I had plans to make lasagna.

The store does not have the requested product, La Brea Bakery Take & Bake Rustic Ciabatta Loaf. Would you like a replacement?

Sure any Take and Bake bread . . .

Thank you <hands praying emoji>

Picture of Take and Bake Talera rolls

Ok great . . . I got you . . . eyes & ears in here lol <wink face emoji>

Eyes and ears in here? What does he mean? I yank the charger cord out of my phone and sit up in bed.

Steve C replaced: La Brea Bakery Take & Bake Rustic Ciabatta Loaf

I get up and head to the bathroom. I bare my teeth in the mirror to check if they're stained from the wine. They look slightly grey through my mouth guard.

The store does not have the requested product, Private Selection Wild Caught Jumbo Lump Crab Meat. Would you like a replacement? Been out of stock for some time

How does he know it's been out of stock? Who is he talking to? I was embarrassed I even added $29.99 lump crab meat to my cart in the first place. *What kind of asshole orders that?* I plead with Steve in my head, *Just refund it and move on.*

Picture of Alaska Delights Wild Alaska Pollock Surimi Seafood

No that's ok. I can skip it

Only thing I see that's not imitation

I finish brushing my teeth and swish with whitening mouthwash counting backwards from 60. I look in the mirror again and my teeth are still grey.

Ok no problem

Steve C refunded: Private Selection Wild Caught Jumbo Lump Crab Meat

It is the day before Christmas Eve and I have a lot of cooking to do this week. I head to the kitchen and remember I never wrapped up the leftover pizza and salad from last night. I smell the yellowing ranch cup before I catch sight of it on the stove. I am nauseated.

The store does not have the requested product, Kowalski Natural Casing Polish Kielbasa. Would you like a replacement?

Picture of Kowalski Smoked Sausage

The Kowalski is great!

I told my son Eli I would make him a Polish dinner—kielbasa, pierogi, sauerkraut, kluski. He's probably on his way home now. I look at the clock on the stove and imagine him driving on the Ohio turnpike. I'm surprised he hasn't texted me to say he's on his way.

Ok great.

Steve C replaced: Kowalski Natural Casing Polish Kielbasa

Eli said he was going to make the trip from Pittsburgh in a single four-hour stretch, not stop to go to the bathroom or get gas. He planned to avoid all contact. I wonder if he changed his mind about traveling. I spot four empty red wine bottles near the side door that are meant for recycling and feel slight relief at the idea of him staying at school.

The store does not have the requested product, Donkey Chips Tortilla Chips, Authentic, Salted. Would you like a replacement?

Unsalted is available only one bag left

Ok I'll take unsalted

Unless you have another preferred brand

Goddammit. I take the pizza box with two hardened slices inside and try to stuff it into a full wastebasket. Something leaks down the side of the trash can. If I bend down to wipe it up I will throw up, so I leave it alone.

Ok great

Steve C replaced: Donkey Chips Tortilla Chips, Authentic, Salted

I start to feel bad for being so annoyed. He's clearly trying. The store is probably packed with shoppers and their lists, barreling through the aisles trying to get the last ingredients they need for Christmas dinner.

No that's good I can salt those boys myself <smiley face emoji>

<Laughing face emoji>

Picture of dried basil

I actually need fresh for a recipe so if they don't have that I can skip it

But thanks

Ok no problem

What are you making ?

I always loved watching people in line at the grocery store unload their shopping carts. As they placed items on the belt I would invent scenarios for them in my head. I can't recall the last time I was at the grocery store. I imagine the cart, my cart, with all of my items, the bread, cheese, sausage, tortilla chips, staring back at him while he rolls down the aisle checking his phone. *Couldn't he figure out what I'm making if he wanted to? Has he invented my story yet?*

Lasagna

Sounds yummy <drooling face emoji>

The store does not have the requested product, Clorox Disinfecting Wipes. Would you like a replacement?

Picture of Redi Wipes

Ok I'll take those!

The store does not have the requested product, Glade Holiday Pine Wonderland Candle. Would you like a replacement?

Picture of shelves lined with blue, pink, cream, and red Glade candles.

I really don't need another pine candle. Such a sad substitute for a Christmas tree.

Any of these to your liking?

No thank you but if they have the Mrs Meyers Pine candles I'll take two of those instead.

Steve C refunded: Glade Holiday Pine Wonderland Candle

I'm trying to wait until these fresh chickens come out so you can have one, I'm just looking around to see where other items could be for you! <Wink face emoji>

Thanks for trying, I really appreciate it!

I look around the kitchen for my purse to see if I have any cash for an extra tip. I mean, he's waiting on fresh chickens, I tell myself. He doesn't have to do that. I pull out a twenty from my wallet and dig around for a pen. I spot a box of holiday cards I ordered a month ago when I had good intentions of sending them out. Next year, I vow. I grab the cards off the top of the refrigerator. I struggle with peeling off the clear stickers that secure either side of the plastic box top, my hands trembling. *Fuck it.* I rip open the box and pluck out an envelope. I imagine myself writing out cards next December and coming up short one envelope.

I'm looking for the Murray's Sharp White Cheddar Cheese. Only 1 was available, however they did have individual wrapped that they cut and wrap here.

Picture of a block of Murray's Sharp White Cheddar

That's great. I'm using it for mac and cheese so gotta have the good stuff!

Would you like two more of these ?

Yes please

Cool . . . making me hungry lol

<Smiley face emoji>

You're seriously the best shopper!

Don't make me smile <blush face emoji>

Lol

Steve C has checked out. We'll send you an update when your order is on the way.

I stuff the twenty dollar bill in the envelope and scribble "Thanks, Steve!" on it then head to the front door. I realize I am braless, still wearing a ridiculous men's oversized Red Wings T shirt and soccer shorts. All told, I probably only owned one proper pair of pajamas in my adult life. When I see pajamas that I like online, I never pull the trigger and order them. I want to be a pajama person, but I somehow always end up with old t-shirts and shorts.

I'm barefoot but open the front door anyway and step out on the porch, working quickly. A blast of cold air hits me and stings. I put the envelope on top of the mailbox along with my ID for the alcohol. I hurry back in, shut and lock the door. I close the shade to the large bay window that overlooks the front porch.

Your Kroger order is on the way!

Delivery estimate is ~11:00am

Your Kroger order will arrive shortly! This order includes alcohol, so please have your ID ready for age verification. For safety, we also sk all shoppers and customers to wear masks t the time of delivery.

A car rumbles in the driveway. I hear a car door slam.

Hi I'm outside . . . Thank you for using Intacart! Please leave me a review. Have a great day!

—Steve C

I stand still in the living room facing the front door. Steve C's on the other side of the door walking to and from his car, placing bag after bag on the porch. I hear the clink of wine bottles and lower-pitched thuds of canned goods, then nothing.

Will do! I left my ID and an xtra tip for you on the mailbox

Ok awesome thank you <blush face emoji>

He grabs the envelope off the mailbox.

If you can just come to the door so I can see your face to match with ID, I had an incident previously don't want that to happen to me again

My heart quickens a little bit. *An incident?* I picture a group of high schoolers ordering a liter of cheap alcohol to be delivered to someone's house one afternoon, maybe a half day of school. Maybe they stole someone's mom's ID from her purse, placing it outside on the mailbox, slipping it back into her purse before she noticed. I imagine Steve C approaching the porch with two bags of alcohol and mixers. Vodka, Mountain Dew. *Did he know?*

Maybe he invited himself in. Can I join you? <smiley face emoji?> When the girls puked it up on the basement floor, did the mom demand to know who bought it, calling all of her daughter's friends until it came out: we got it on Instacart. No, they didn't make us

come to the door. The shopper's name was Steve C.

I can't possibly open the door looking like this and without my mask. It also occurs to me that I have been placing delivery orders of alcohol for months and haven't been asked to come to the door.

I pull back the shade and see a man standing on the porch looking down at his phone, my driver's license resting on top of it. I tap on the window and wave. He's wearing a black jacket and brown ski hat. He nods and smiles and holds up my ID. I shout thanks through the window and close the shade again. I listen for footsteps back to his car, the door slamming.

My cell phone vibrates again. I pick it up from the coffee table where I left it.

You and your family have a happy holiday. You do have a great personality.

I hear his car still running. He hasn't left the driveway yet. I imagine him staring down at his phone, waiting on my reply.

Great personality! I laugh to myself. That thing you say about someone who isn't attractive. I think back to the time a high school boyfriend told my sister that he wished he could mash my personality with another girl's looks, then he would have the perfect girlfriend. I never cared that he said that. It made me feel interesting, somehow proof I wasn't shallow or vapid.

I hear the car still running. I start typing thank you but decide against it. I settle on You too!

I hear the faint rumble of the engine grow fainter as he reverses out of the driveway then drives down the street, out of sight.

Doug Nufer

a raven

once in on a noir eve eerie as i swore in reverie
over numerous or curious scenes in some inane memoir
as i was soon anear a snooze i was aware via some cues
some nervous susurrus issues, issues in a murmur on a roar
—a newcomer—i came aware—now arises in a roar,
some newcomer, or someone more.

o, i'm sure in reminiscence, i was in a season vicious
as some crass incense is miasmic in a reservoir.
insecure, i saw a morrow, in vain saw surcease of sorrow
in scenes common as a corn row, sorrow o'er once mine, enore,
a so rare evanescence essence an eminence names as enore
unseen moreover evermore.

so a morose, suave, unsure sense in some screen move in crimson
wore me, sore me, in an insane scare in no encore.
so i, as visions come immerse me, mimic a coercive swami
—some caravan commissioner or service man i'm sure
some caravan insomniac or service man i'm sure
is ever even or no more.

soon i came in on a resource, a carom in a veer, a recourse
—sir or ma'am, i reassure, excuse me as i vow manure
swoons as i was in a snooze, so some innocuous muse
as innocence arose a ruse accrues a rumor room or on a roar
as i was so sure someone were near—come in, swine ass—i swore
so i see, i see no more.

in visions i saw weave noir, a scare wove me in awe, a scar
i wore in raves no man as i ever saw come as evermore
moreover resonance was mum as no sonorous sum
amasses in a vacuum scrum; as a murmur came in—enore . . .
as i swore in coax me voices came an answer now—enore.
a mere murmur, ere no more.

in mine own room recess remove, i was anxious as an ooze
once more came in inner views raucous as a moose or more
—sure, o, sure—i rose in answer—one more amorous romancer
come in, screw me, necromancer, so our secrecies can score

reassure me now in answer, so our reveries can soar—
evanescence came, no more.

now as i overcame a screen, concurrences arose: a scene
seen scarce, a raven, one eminence as vicars swore
no minimum concern on me, no anxious move as some careen
more in insouciance serene, a raven now rose over me
arose in a narcissus move o'er me as romeos arouse o'er censors
arose immune versus marm scissors.

as a rara avis circus can amuse me, recuse curses
via onerous immersion in a reverie we wore
—as a crown is worn, a maven, i am sure, is never craven
as some sorrow's vicious raven asea as on a man-o-war
answer me, i crave a name sir as i sense a unicorn—
caw a raven—nevermore.

as a rex crow can amaze me in eerie common summaries
in nonsense answers, reveries can seem in vain or mean no more
so we convene as women, men, in our communion unison,
no one, save me, ever renew a croon, a raven score
as moors a scow in a marina over rivers run a course
we can name as nevermore.

so a raven, one mass avis over me arose one access
monomaniacs converse in as scarce as a one moan encore
no excessive mezzo music, no coo in a mesozoic
resonance as microcosmic macaroni sauces roar
as i re-ran in a murmur, —raven moves on soon, i am sore—
caw a raven —nevermore.

anxious as a session ceases via answer in mimesis
—sure—i reason—as a raven mimics via memories, encores
resonance re: verses voices; curses serve as no eunoias,
re-run miseries' auroras, movie consumer omnivores
reconceive in ceremonies screams envision scenes ere more
as in never nevermore.

now a raven reassures me ever in amicus curie
as assessors can concern me, i arose secure in rumor
i in innocence, naive was common sense's reason sneezes
on a run i came unconscious as an omen's raven swore
in a mercenariness encore
means in a caw on—nevermore.

so i was aswarm in seizure as no answers came as we swerve
on incarcere as an avaricious eminence wore
over us secure, invasive, i assume as in immersive
in a mire so aversive as an evanescence rose o'er
in a vision i envision in monomania once more
e. revives me nevermore.

now i sense a new aroma in an unseen censer coma
as some conscious nemesis comes as an osmosis cures a sore
—scum—i scream—a carcinoma venomous consumes a soma
as i unwaver in zen om a reminiscence, o enore
cram, consume a new erosion, overcome, inure versus enore
caw a raven—nevermore.

—seer, vicious crow, or vermin—i assess as i examine.
—can a reason cause our union or are we casino scores,
cameos in ceremonies insincere announcer emcees
croon in comic reveries, unconscious corrosive encores
come, assure me, answer, cure me, raise me in omniscience, soar—
caw a raven—nevermore.

—seer, vicious crow, or vermin—i aver or re-examine
—as our cosmos oversees us in omniscience, our amour
nurse me in an ozone sorrow, reassure me as i winnow
memories in vain so narrow in a maze i muse on, one enore
save me as i swoon in care, o, in communion cameo enore
caw a raven—nevermore.

—caw au revoir in ceremonies, crow or vermin—i, in moan, ease
a reverse course as i murmur—scram, vamoose, rise in a soar
sow no omen as a souvenir or reminiscence so anear
me in an ominous veneer, scram, vamoose, so caw au revoir
now remove a razor, ow, mon coeur; scram, crow, vamoose, croon no encore.
caw a raven—nevermore.

so a raven, no remover, now as ever is a viewer
in a ceremonious oasis on nirvana rumor
as in mien an evanescence ever more accrues an essence
reassures me in senescence as a crow remains in manor
as i reassure in essence mine can now on no soar o'er,
raise i ever . . . nevermore.

Stephen Moles

Pure Meaning

From *Your Dark Meaning Mouse*
(Sagging Meniscus, Nov. 2021)

In 2016, a team of dark meaning researchers embarked on a time-consuming and potentially life-consuming experiment to see if they could produce a quantity of 100% pure meaning in the DMRI's secret underground liboratory.[1] They took the biography of Stephen Moles as their prima materia and subjected it to an intense and prolonged literary-alchemical procedure in order to break down the surface details and cause its hidden properties to emerge.

Over the next two years, the biographical material passed through seven distinct stages, from calcination to coagulation, and eventually became the mysterious substance known as darkmethyltryptameaning, which has a number of paradoxical properties such as superintroreflectivity and apparently infinite importance along with utter incomprehensibility.

Although Stephen Moles donated his literal meaning for the experiment, leaving him in the unfortunate situation of no longer making any sense to anyone, and therefore able to look forward to only the most wretched kind of literary career, the resulting material was so refined that it contained no traces whatsoever of any personal significance.

This product was not some low-grade concoction tainted with the peculiarities of its producer, or a cheap, watery knockoff with about as much meaning in it as the average inkjet printer cartridge; this was pure sense, it was self-supporting symbolism, alive and fully conscious of its role as the substance of all stories and the antidote to insignificance.

The only thing that linked the pure meaning to the literally dead author[2] who helped to produce it was the fact that it was later exhibited at an event in London which also saw the launch of the writer's new book along with a surreal enactment of his erasure from the surface of Flatland.

It was on February 23rd 2018, in a psychiatric hospital near King's Cross, that the darkmethyltryptameaning made its first ever public appearance. It was thought that the visitors needed to be protected from the dangerously high levels of paradoxicality given off by the substance just as much as the substance needed to be protected from them; therefore the entire time it was on show, the arcane solution was held in a small flask which was in turn housed in a larger glass dome. It was, however, quite easy for all members of the public who stood within close proximity of the "philosopher's fluid" to feel its extraordinary effects.

The pure meaning's sphere of influence is in fact thought to have extended beyond the walls of the hospital since there were reports from several local residents of a mysterious humming sound, which was accompanied, in one case, by the appearance of bright orbs in the sky. It was at close range, however, that the effects were most apparent, with some guests describing how the liquid seemed to move and sparkle in response to their voice or thoughts, and others explaining how they felt the gravity of the situation increase dramatically, to the point where they seemed to be at the centre of a huge black hole.

However fantastical it may seem to others, the experience of each individual is a true reflection of the subjectively objective reality of the darkmethyltryptameaning. Those who burst into tears at the sight of it, those who experienced fits of uncontrollable laughter in its presence, those who revered it and those who ridiculed it—all of them came equally close to an understanding of the most substantial substance known to man, and all were united in their differences.

Despite a whole host of positive experiences being registered by those present, a moment of disaster occurred sometime towards the end of the evening. While Stephen Moles was enacting his death for the patients and visitors inside St Pancras Hospital, someone snatched the glass container and ran off with the world's only quantity of pure meaning. It is not known for certain who made away with the priceless exhibit but there are two obvious suspects, since on CCTV footage taken from outside the hospital a short while before the theft was discovered, a couple of men wearing satchels and long black leather coats could be seen darting out of the building and speeding off into the night on motorcycles.

It also remains a distinct possibility, in light of the uniqueness of the item, that it was stolen to order.

There are many possible uses for darkmethyl-tryptameaning, some of them favourable to humankind, others simply too dreadful to mention, but every possible application, whatever the intention of the experimenter, comes with a great deal of uncertainty and therefore also much danger.

Even those who have spent their entire lives researching meaning are still in the dark about the vast majority of its properties, so anyone who thinks they can mess around with it and not risk bringing about a cataclysmic event for humanity is, quite simply, a fool.

The Dark Meaning Research Institute is appealing for the return of this extremely dangerous material and is offering a reward of £10,000 to anyone who can provide information that leads to its recovery. You can email them confidentially via darkmeaningresearchinstitute@gmail.com or leave an anonymous note in the hollow of any oak tree in Great Britain and they will receive it in due course.

---

1. In all previous attempts by the DMRI and others, purity levels of no higher than 64% had ever been reached.

2. Literally dead in the sense that his literality had ceased to exist, which is both the most literal death possible and, paradoxically, a type of rebirth.

Marvin Cohen

Cohen's Useful Directions

LITERARY ADVICE (DIALOGUE)

In order to be able to write better original poetry and prose, do you recommend going a little crazy?

That's an idle question in your case, because you're ALREADY crazy.

No, let's be serious. Enough alcohol or strong coffee can twist mental images into original patterns, thus affording unusual turns of inspiration.

That's true. But don't become addicted to alcohol in a way that you lose track of good reasoning in word selection, warping your judgement.

I want to get violent combinations of warring images.

All right, but avoid dangerous drugs and excessive inebriation.

Are you a "moderation" prig?

Plato and Aristotle endorsed the art of moderation.

Those Greeks lived too long ago. To hell with them. I'm modern, at all costs.

But being modern doesn't cost you a penny. It's free, and comes with the territory.

I want to write with such originality that publishers will be desperate to publish me.

Certain types of publishers are too "commercial" to consider publishing you. Only try for so-called "literary" publishers.

Thanks for the tips, which if they pay off, I'll give you a free copy of my first publication.

Holding my breath isn't mandatory, so I'll resist it.

TRYING TO FOOL DEATH / PANTINGLY DRAINS YOUR BREATH

Death is hardly easy to cheat.
I offer him bread and say, "It's whole wheat."
But he'll say, "I want whole grain.
Now I'll enter you with extra pain
for trying to fool me.
Trifling with me at your expense
requests the penalty I dispense
to you for being a wise guy.
If you resist, I'll make you cry
in such a way that the tears will flow
to your whole tomb below.
All your mourners will get the drizzle,
as your bones rot with extra fizzle
like a big town under a missile."
That was the end of me.
I lit up like a Christmas tree
and smiled my adieu to Life,
but all the lights blanked out,
doffed by Death to dim any doubt.
My loss was a one-sided rout,
with no signs of a return bout.

YOUR UNIQUE STYLE / SHINED FOR A WHILE, / BEFORE JOINING THE RUBBISH PILE

Life is a wonderful treat
if you excel in "the social beat."
Be the most popular man in town
and achieve some special renown.
Everybody enjoys your company
and invites you to a meal free
(acknowledging your poverty).
So you don't have to pay a cent
to be socially "in" one hundred percent.
They love you eccentrically dressed,
which is a loud attempt to impress.
They even enjoy your puns,
and celebrate your famous wit.
You and society temporarily fit.
But don't get old too quick.
Youth was a divine sparkle,
and your company was in demand.
Women loved to throng around you.
Philosophers loved to expound you,
and make theories that devolve
into how well life's problems you solve.
Perhaps you were a sheer genius.
Society took you up
and made you drink from a golden cup.
However, they kept you in poverty,
because that was your special property.
But your popularity is splashed away
when creaky old age bends you in two,
and society requires a sensation that's new,
creating a wild fashion that's overdue.
You disappear from "everyone's" expired view.

David Winner

Shrunk

1.

Five steps out towards the sidewalk, then up to the porch of Joel's house. I regard the out-of-date signs. Guard Dog and Beware of Dog when there is no dog. Four names are typed on a yellowed card when only Joel still lives here. And he has been gone for months and may never return. Missing from the list is the only being present in the house. Sweetie, the elderly cat who I have been tasked with feeding.

The stench hits me as I open the door. My facemask barely dulls it. A sickly-sweet miasma of cooking smells, animal urine and mold. The floors and counters are sticky with grease. There can't really be Covid, though, unless I brought it there myself the last time I was inside.

Sweetie soon makes her appearance, mewing plaintively. A pretty grey girl with matted hair, she wriggles her back when I kneel down and pet her. A Kaspar Hauser of a cat, she's spent much of her life exiled to the basement.

Stroking her back, I listen for voices in the empty house. Recently, I've learned one of its secrets and witnessed one of its darker moments.

The forsaken block onto which my wife, Angela, and I moved in the summer of 2018 lies in Brooklyn on the far side of Kensington near Coney Island Avenue, a heavily trafficked thoroughfare even during Covid, replete with car parts dealers, extermination suppliers and Bengali banquet halls.

Soon after our arrival, we'd realized that we had joined a five-house stretch of house owned by white people between the Nigeria church on the corner and the Jamaican family two doors down from us.

The American flag, multiple motorcycle and ramshackle porch suggest some rougher character, but Joel next door is generall mild-mannered. Extremely short, a little bi pudgy and 77 years old, he is plagued by ill heath and still grieves his wife, who died ove a decade ago.

While Joel is soulful, melancholic, hi neighbor on the opposite side from us Adrian, is buoyant, preternaturally cheerful Her dog, Charlie, barks fiercely but is sweet natured whereas ours, Hazel, looks decep tively friendly. Ethnicity figures in the story Adrian is Italian-American, her father immi grating from Naples whereas Joel's fathe came from Cuba and adopted Joel's mother' Jewish faith.

2.

In the spring of 2019, Joel rejoined the sororal/fraternal dog-owners association of East 7th Street when his sister (living in a Chassidic community upstate) wanted to get rid of her dog, Tazzy, named after the Tasmanian devil. Joel soon became besotted with the elderly little creature, whose fur was covered in knots and rashes and whose kidneys were gradually failing. Often during the day while I was writing or reading, I would hear Joel chatting amiably with Tazzy. And occasionally, if he was feeling sprightly enough Tazzy yelping back.

The following spring, not long after the virus hit, the liquor store for which Joel worked part-time closed then reopened without hiring him back. Suddenly stir-crazy, he was taking more and more joy rides on his two-wheeled vehicles when he was run over by a car on Ocean Parkway and busted his knee, leaving him hospitalized for weeks, not ambulatory for months. He could recuperate with his sister upstate, but it was our job to care for his animals.

Angela was the first to brave his cluttered house to mix wet dog food with water and canine kidney meds and shoot them into Tazzie's mouth with a syringe. And feed poor Sweetie, who had finally escaped the basement.

Angela's fear of a solitary old age got exacerbated by Joel's house. She pictured herself and worse me (no Joel but messy) if we got predeceased, a filthy, miserable old age. Thankfully, Adrian and I began to share the burden with her.

The poor animal, who'd been so lovingly cared for, was now entirely alone except for our brief visits. Tazzy, it should be noted, did not seem interested or capable of walking up and down the block as he had with Joel in better days. Rather, he used the backyard for a bathroom while Sweetie, as always, had the entire basement for her litter box. Our care was a stop-gap measure. We were nothing like Joel.

Late on a Tuesday evening about a month after Joel's accident, our own dog started barking savagely. Adrian was knocking on our living room window. Something was wrong next door.

Breathless, we joined her outside, then poured into Joel's living room. Tazzy lay motionless in Joel's chair, but when we got closer, we could see that he was faintly breathing.

I thought about doctors, for animals and for people, hospitals, medical tests. Not long before hospitals had locked down, I had accompanied a friend to hear devastating news from an oncologist.

Nothing like that was available in Joel's living room, but the three of us knew without consulting anyone that Tazzy was dying. The question was what to do.

Not call Joel. Immobile upstate with his relatives, he could not race in in the middle of the night to catch his beloved creature's dying breaths. He could only fret. He could only suffer.

Hours before the death of our very sick cat two summers before, he'd emitted alarming guttural sounds unlike anything we had ever heard, discordant despair. Of course, we got him to the animal hospital where (the cliché seemed apt) they put him out of his misery.

But Tazzy lay peacefully on Joel's chair.

He hardly reacted when Adrian picked him up and started to rock him in her arms.

Except his penis stuck out, erect in his dying.

"Look," said Adrian, "his little pipinello."

Then she blanched, embarrassed by both the genital reference and the sudden Italian. But years with Angela (whose father was from Sorrento) had taught me some basic expressions.

"Pipinello," I repeated to reassure her.

Then shit started draining from Tazzy onto her shirt. Saddened rather than disgusted, she put him back on Joel's chair, and we made a date for eight the following morning. The three of us would gather, then return to Joel's.

I guess it was the shadow of death. That evening before sleeping I remembered a nap that I had taken years before in my childhood bedroom while visiting my parents with Angela. My mother was dying of Parkinson's in a room across the hall.

Delicately, Angela had awoken me. The hospice nurse had said that the end was near.

My father, myself and Angela sat by my mother's bed lightly touching her while she struggled to breathe.

We gathered outside of Joel's door the following morning. For some inexplicable reason, I wanted to be the first to enter and find out what happened with Tazzy.

But Adrian was faster. From her body language as she approached him, we could tell that no surprises were in store.

She lifted his stiff body and lightly shook it.

"Tazzy, Tazzy," she declared in her old school Brooklyn accent, "come back to us, Tazzy." Then she put him back on Joel's chair. "He's gone," she whispered, "he's gone."

3.

Later, outside the house, Angela called Joel. Her face looked intent as we listened to the sound of the phone ringing and Joel picking up with his usual avuncular tone.

I thought about different bad news that Joel had received, the moment that he learned of his wife's cancer diagnosis, the moment he knew that she was not going to make it.

After asking Joel how he was and calmly listening to his response, Angela told him that she had "something that I have to tell you, something sad."

"Tazzy has died."

"What??!! How??!!" Joel could not accept what he'd just heard. But soon we heard the sounds of sobbing on the other end. Later would come anger, recrimination. But firs was only sorrow.

That afternoon Joel had a doctor's appointment in Brooklyn, and his niece had driven him to the house beforehand. Rather than to hobble inside on a broken knee, he directed us from the back of her car.

It was unclear what we would do with Tazzy. Joel wanted to see the evidence of the terrible news that he'd learned that morning. I had been reading Julia Leigh's gothic about a woman clinging for weeks to her swaddled still-born baby, and I wondered whether Joel wanted to take Tazzy with him, carrying him around as a morbid talisman.

I was in our kitchen, I think, when a text arrived on my phone, Angela from next door. I was wanted. They needed me to dig a hole for Tazzy in Joel's backyard.

Adrian took me inside and found me a shovel. Then she carefully appraised the weeds and detritus strewn everywhere.

She showed me exactly where to dig. I had to be careful not to exhume any of the dogs and cats buried by Joel in different places in his yard.

Thankfully, Tazzy was tiny. It wouldn't be so much work, and I could easily stick to a limited area. So I pitched my shovel into the greyish dirt, depositing what I had dug up into a heap nearby, lying on top, most probably, of some long-dead creature.

Just as I was finishing, my phone rang, Angela again. Joel wanted to take Tazzy to a vet to have him cremated instead. I don't think he was ready to part with the body.

It was barely afternoon. The day had crept slowly forward. Only a few hours before, we had discovered the body.

I carefully scattered the dirt back over the hole that I had created.

When I got back to the front of house, I saw that Joel's niece had left Joel in the car and was standing next to Adrian. Angela approached her. And made the suggestion that had been on all of our minds. Could some sort of expert deep cleaner be paid to improve the condition of Joel's house while he was away, so he could return to someplace healthier and safer? The filth bothered him too. We knew it did.

"He's not coming back," were her ominous words.

As if Joel had been kidnapped into Chasidim. The week before Joel had apologized to Angela for not calling her back from Friday until Sunday. He could not charge his phone over the sabbath. Though he was not at all that type of Jew.

4.

After Joel and his niece have left, Angela, Adrian and I stand in front of the house. And Adrian starts to give us some of Joel's backstory.

Back back backstory.

When she had first met him some fifty years ago, he had been living in the same house with his first wife, a "tough little Italian lady," according to Adrian who was a bigger, softer example.

One evening not so many years after meeting Joel, Adrian had gone to the movies with her husband, Angelo, and had seen Joel's tough Italian wife, flirting openly with another man.

"A black guy," Adrian had explained.

"Colored?" she had asked, struggling for the right expression.

"Black," Angela and I insisted.

"Right, black matters," said Adrian, getting the term right, not endorsing the movement.

And soon Joel's first wife was no longer living next door.

Not long after that, Adrian ran into wife number one, and wife number one had felt that an explanation was owed.

"Joel," she explained, "had shrunk."

Someone to whom I later told the story brought up the racial penis-size mythology, but I don't think it was about Joel's penis.

Something about all the working-class white families, which must have encompassed the whole block back then, and the blocks surrounding it. Something about all the nearly identical houses right next to each other, some feeling of restriction. Something about Joel's absolute control over his domain, which was about to start disassembling.

I stop petting Sweetie and go over to the cat food cans piled haphazardly on a dining room table used for storage for decades.

While continuing to think about the sounds the walls must have heard.

What Joel said to the first wife and first wife back to Joel when she had been leaving him.

Wife number two's last days. Why did she have to leave, Joel had once asked Angela, his voice dripping with anger.

Joel is back at the house now, mobile enough to shuffle slowly back and forth to the stores on Coney Island Avenue. Since Tazzy's demise, he's devoted himself to Sweetie. At all hours of the day, we hear him reassuring her, scolding her, explaining things to her as he's been doing with all the creatures, animal and human, that have inhabited his house since he purchased it in the seventies.

Colin Gee

Dear John

As you have probably already suspected, I am writing to tell you that I can no longer see you. You have become so small that you are literally not visible to me anymore. Even if I could locate you and hear your voice—and I write this knowing that you are probably still somewhere in the apartment—I would be afraid of hurting you with my big fingers.

Maybe that is the real crux of the problem. You made me feel fat, John. I am a little woman with a flat tummy, and you made me feel fat and gross! And I can't go on without seeing you.

It would be one thing if we had grown small together, slowly shrinking at a constant and equal rate over the course of the past five or six months so that our kisses were always the same size. You know me John and know it isn't about the physical, but of course I miss that too. And what was strange and unsatisfying for me must have been terrifying, even revolting for you.

It's too bad because there was a day about three months ago when you were the perfect size for me, a pint-sized little John, and I know I could have loved you forever like that.

The worst thing is that now I am afraid that I may be ruined for other men. After what we had, how do you expect me to go back to their sloppy fat kisses and banana-sized fingers?

You were so unbelievably adorable and I loved you.

Given your tiny size I have written this with the smallest scrunched-up little script I could so that it won't take you forever to read it. I imagine you, running back and forth across the page, trying to remember what the last letter was, taking hours to decipher a single sentence. I don't know what you will do when you finally manage to read t the end. I don't want you to cry or kill yoursel even though it probably doesn't matter.

I mean, how long do you think you can con tinue to shrink without disappearing com pletely? The last time we talked, over the week end, I was able to see your mouth move with th aid of a magnifying glass but I couldn't hear an of the words you were saying. It was just like What? What, John? I admit that it has been funn to hear the pitch of your voice getting higher an higher day after day, but that turns out not t have been as ridiculous as not hearing it at all. I was at that moment I realized I couldn't keep pre tending that you weren't gone. That there was n point in trying to get back the size ratio we had.

Will there come a day when you can't see your self? You're already dead to me, John, but hov much longer do you have before you are the size of a bacteria, and how will you defend yoursel from all the nasty germs in this disgusting apart ment? You're going to wish you hadn't been such a slob when you were bigger.

I still have dreams about us and the plans we made. If you had stopped shrinking for only a few months I could have taken you to Italy in my suitcase. It wouldn't have cost anything to take you out either. You always were a lightweight but the last few times we drank together you couldn' even finish one beer.

I loved spending time with you, listening to you breathe next to me, smelling your body close to mine. But now I can't see or smell you. Maybe you are close to me right now. Maybe you are on me, like a tick or a weird rash.

I want to see you, John, but only so I don't step on you or vacuum you up. This is goodbye. As you may or may not already know, I have a new boyfriend and he's coming over in a couple of hours. I would appreciate it if you're off me before then.

Isabela

Tyler C. Gore

December 26

From *My Life of Crime*
(Sagging Meniscus, Sept. 2022)

This is always a special day for me. Oh, I know, it's Boxing Day, and even though I'm an American, I'll be obliged to entertain guests today, because my wife Natasha is from Trinidad—once a far-flung corner of the British Empire—and she shares the British delusion that Boxing Day is an actual holiday. It's basically like an off-brand Christmas. We'll have a big lunch with relatives we didn't see on Christmas Day and exchange gifts, which—although no one will officially admit it—are often re-gifts, an opportunity for everyone to fob off their disappointments and rejects from the day before: novelty pens, electric pasta forks, holiday-themed pajamas. So I haven't fully emerged from the woodchipper of the holiday season yet. But I'm feeling a kind of buoyancy, a sense of gratitude and wonder, the way you might if you'd just escaped a burning building.

I must confess I am one of those people who does not like Christmas. More accurately: I *loathe* Christmas. I dread its hateful approach, and every year, starting in November, I am seized by fits of Yuletide rage, and compulsively subject my poor wife—who loves Christmas, as all decent people do—to spasms of outraged, spittle-flecked invective regarding the Season To Be Fucking Jolly.

I don't like the gift-giving, which requires planning and shopping, two activities I find unenjoyable and anxiety-producing, and then there's the preemptive matter of advising other people what they should give to *me*, which I also don't like, because the things I would actually like to receive are either trivial and utilitarian (a large carton of Home Depot garbage bags, or a new filter for our air purifier) or they are big-ticket technology items (a fancy gazillion-pixel DSLR camera; a faster, sleeker laptop uncrippled by porn viruses) that are too expensive to ask anyone to purchase on my behalf.

I don't care for gingerbread houses, elves, or plastic reindeer, and I can't stand the horrid music, which unpleasantly evokes the polo shirts and missionary positions of the Eisenhower Era, and by Christmas Day I've been forced to endure those two dozen canonical songs in every public space for nearly two months. Santa Claus is vaguely pedophiliac and also just plain stupid. The geographically-disadvantaged toy workshop presents obvious logistical issues, the invasive tracking of naughty-or-nice metrics violates any number of European privacy laws, and a fat old man who insists upon delivering gifts by cramming himself down smoking chimneys sounds like a surefire candidate for the Darwin Awards. I'm sorry, Virginia, but Santa is a slapdash assemblage of codswallop foisted upon gullible children by corporate advertisers, and your friends are right to scorn you. I wish we had a Krampus tradition in this country, a malignant, leering, red-eyed Krampus prancing behind an enormous coal-black phallus, a truly pagan Krampus who would induce brain-exploding seizures of Puritanical outrage in Fox News commentators every December. *That* would be something to be merry about.

I would prefer to spend Christmas as the Jews do. With other Jews. In a Chinese restaurant, followed by a movie. Every year, I devote resentful hours of thought to the liberating possibility of converting to Judaism, but no one would take me seriously—I just want to be *Jewish*, not *a practicing Jew*—and besides, my conversion would just saddle me with all sorts of additional social obligations, and the goyim would still make me do Christmas.

Admittedly, I do like Midnight Mass. I'm not much of a churchgoer, but I like the warm darkness and the flickering candles, the organ and the choir and the majestic Baroque carols, the big-hearted solemnity of gathering together with strangers in a place that is not sports arena or a bar. I like Christmas trees, too. That's a lovely tradition. The evergreen scent, the lights, the gold and red.

Oh, but the *presents*. The presents ruin everything. They look nice under the tree, all the fancy wrapping and ribbons, but why can't they just be symbolic? One year I came up with the idea that everyone should just give each other figs. You know, those clever little circular packages of dried figs they sell at the supermarket? Everyone likes figs. They are cheap, they are nutritious, and they are vaguely Biblical. You wouldn't have to wrap them because everyone would know that you are giving them figs, but you could wrap them if you felt like it. Re-gifting figs would be a breeze.

Because it wears you down, the sheer ugliness of the frenzied consumerism. Charlie Brown was right to be troubled by it. Christmas is supposed to be a season when you take stock of your shitty selfish nature and think of the less fortunate for a change—*peace on earth and goodwill to men*—but it's just an orgy of thoughtless greed. Gimme gimme gimme. Xbox. iPhone. Roomba. Fifty-five inch flatscreen with five-speaker Surround Sound so you can watch George Bailey sacrifice ambition and opportunity for the sake of community service in high-definition OLED. Like, not to shit on anyone's parade, but there's an Australia-sized wad of plastic crap floating in the Pacific, the fish are dying out, the glaciers are melting, and polar bear cubs are floating off into the sea. I don't want to be the tree-hugging sourpuss at the holiday party who whines, Come on, people, think of the planet—but *Come on, people, think of the planet! Why won't you merry-making assholes think of the planet??*

But what I hate most about Christmas, the real underlying nugget of radioactive hatred, is that it is socially obligatory. *You are not allowed to opt out.* Think about it. You can opt out of birthday parties. You can even opt out of your own birthday (It's delightful.) You can opt out of dinner dates, dentist appointments, and poetry readings. You can opt out of weddings—that's what RSVPs are for. You can opt out of funerals and send flowers instead. But you can't opt out of Christmas. Even if you try—and I have—you will just sit by yourself in an eerily quiet apartment subjected to Dickensian visitations from the Ghost of Christmas Guilt, and you'll wind up spending the whole day feeling resentful and sorry for yourself because you have to spend Christmas Day alone. And so, against my will, I will be be dragged away from all the things I need to do or like to do, forced to lug shopping bags of laboriously wrapped gifts on busses trains airplanes so that I may ritualistically distribute these perfunctory and unnecessary consumer goods to various relatives, and I must in turn receive items I do not want or need which will take up precious space in my apartment, I will overeat pie eggnog nuts fruitcake because I have no self-control, I will gain ten pounds and spend the rest of the year trying to lose five of them, I will have to keep up the exhausting pretense that I am brimming with joy because this the Happiest Time of The Year and everyone will strain to be painfully nice to one another because no one wants to spoil Christmas because *spoiling Christmas* is the moral equivalent of *kicking a puppy.*

Whew. Okay, okay, deep breath.

All of this is undeniably true, but . . .

Christmas is *over*.

It often takes me all of January to recover from it.

The rage, the shame. The apologies.

Only 364 days to go.

John Patrick Higgins

Silvia

I tried to focus on the fuzzy, busy objects that circled my head like a halo of flies. Breathing in dead leaves and desiccated insects, I felt ʰem settle in my lungs like dust in a crypt. This ʷas not my beautiful mouth. This was not my ʰeautiful tongue. The latter was a snake's belly ʳiding over ruins. What had happened?

Something rolled off the bed and fell with a ʰuted clunk onto the carpet. It was a bottle. And I ᵊmembered: it had been Christmas Day. I had ʰeen drinking.

I ran my mouth under the cold tap. Life sprang ᵖp as though on a dusty alien world, my terᵃformed tongue blooming, becoming flexible ʰnd exploratory. I spat into the sink and tannin ᵊdiment coloured the saliva like sick blood. I was ʰive. I resolved to fry an egg in butter and open a ʰn of fat Coke.

I had survived another Christmas day alone, ʰut this was to be a sterner test: it was the day of my ʰnnual visit to my aunt Silvia.

Silvia lived in three rooms of a large house on ʰe other side of town. She had red hair and had ʰudied ballet, and I think her Sixties had been ʰildly bohemian—she'd married an airline pilot, ʰnd there were rumours in the family she'd enterʰined gentlemen callers during his long-haul ʰights. She'd been a sort of low rent Princess Marʰaret in our household mythology, but now all that ʷas left of the family was me, and I wasn't scanʰalised—I was traumatised. To see her I was going ʰ have to drive across town.

I threw up and brushed my teeth and sprayed ʰyself with a lot of deodorant to disguise the hand ʰanitizer funk emanating from every pore.

At the front door, I pressed my head against the cool glass and stared into the grey glow of the morning. Then I staggered to the car, and once more savoured the delicious chill as I placed hands and cheek against its freezing chassis. Refreshed, I let myself in and started her up. I made it fifty yards down the road before pulling over and running back to the house to see if I had closed the front door, which I hadn't. I trudged back to the car, which was ticking over in clouds of condensation, the driver's door open.

I let my hands and feet do the driving and did not engage at all, knowing that if my brain blundered into proceedings there would be a major traffic incident. It would have been like those moments of frozen confusion I encountered in typing up notes, where my brain overtook my hands, and I no longer knew where the semicolon key was. Besides, I was already using my brain to sustain a gentle, fizzing panic. I scanned the landscape for signs of the police, squinting at dark shapes in the cold eye of the rear-view mirror.

I wouldn't ordinarily have driven at all. I had been asleep and drunk an hour ago and would clearly fail a breathalyser test. But I was late, it was Boxing Day and Silvia could be very fierce. I hoped the police would be at home with their families. Of course, there were probably lonely and unhappy policemen, policemen like me, who had no families and were likely to be vindictive, because they were working during the holidays and nobody loved them, so I kept constant, paranoid surveillance while my hands and feet got on with the job of not actually killing anybody. It worked. I got to Silvia's house ten minutes after I said I would, and I had not been arrested.

"Christ. You smell like a brewery."

I released Silvia from my embrace. She was brittle and neat, her hair still suspiciously red, her face caked in powder. She wore a baby blue cardigan, pearl earrings, and her eyes were bright in the gypsum mask of her face. She left an imprint in dust on the front of my raincoat, like the Veronica.

"I can't believe you drove. You stink like a dosser. "

"Thanks very much," I said. "I smell death on you."

"Charming as ever, though you're probably right. I'm properly on my last legs now."

I draped my coat over the end of the banister. She picked it up with a tut, placed it on a coat-stand and, with a balled tissue retrieved from her sleeve, attempted to scrub her face powder from my lapel with spit. I went straight into the kitchen, slipped on her pinnie and five minutes later I was crushing fennel seeds with a mortar and pestle. She appeared armed with two large tumblers of gin and tonic and two small paper hats.

We had been doing this every year for the last decade, after I'd got back in touch with her follow-ing Mum's funeral. The family had always been small but by the time I'd reached my forties it had dwindled to nothing. Silvia had a son in Australia she didn't talk to, and I had a couple of cousins in America I'd never met. Her husband and my par-ents were long gone, so this was it. Every Boxing Day I came to her house, cooked a chicken, the only thing I cooked well, and then we got drunk to-gether in front of the television. After dinner the bickering would start, my character would be swiftly atomised, and I would threaten to leave but I never did because she kept a good cellar, and my house was miles away. So, I took the constructive criticism until she fell asleep with her mouth open, and then fished her false teeth out so she wouldn't choke, placing them on the coffee table in front of her. Then I would drink quietly on my own, watching TV with the sound down until I also fell asleep. Every year for a decade we did this. I didn't mind. She never remembered the harsh-ness of her words. Or maybe she did? There was always faint embarrassment in the morning. She

could remember something, but perhaps she wasn't sure what it was.

I zested a lemon.

"Are you seeing anyone?" said Silvia.

"That question comes earlier every year," I said. "You usually wait until I've finished eating."

"That's a no then?"

"That's a no then."

She prodded my belly. "It's because of this."

"Do you want me to continue cooking you a din-ner? I don't have to do this, you know. I could be at home right now nursing a bad hangover."

"I'm not being cruel, Paul. I say it because I love you."

I stopped zesting the lemon.

"You love me?"

"I have to. You're my last relation."

"You've got a son."

"He's a little shit."

I shook my head. "No, Silvia, I'm not seeing any-one."

"I expect you've missed the boat now," she said sadly. I chopped the garlic.

Dinner was civilized. We drank Pinot Grigio with the bird and listened to a CD of carols sung by The King's Singers. The conversation was polite and dull. Neither of us did much and we had few common interests, so there were lengthy gaps which was fine. The silences were comfortable, and the chicken was good, so there was no need for chat. The paper hats rustled as we chewed, shivering like butterfly wings over our heads.

After dinner we watched television. Our televi-sion watching was an evolved experience, a well-worn rut. Silvia was old and thin and felt the cold, so the heating was fierce, and she was slightly deaf, so the TV volume was blasting, the adverts on com-mercial channels punishingly so.

She narrated each programme, often over ex-pository passages which she found boring, so I was briefed on the action that we had both just seen, but by the middle of the film neither of us had any idea what was going on.

Silvia had a memory for faces but not names, so every time a new person appeared on screen I was asked "Who is he? I know him." If I were able to answer the question, she disagreed with me. "Don't be so stupid. He has a much thinner face." She was bewildered by the end credits when it was revealed that I was correct, wondering how I'd pulled off this feat of legerdemain.

She didn't differentiate between film eras: every film was happening in one big cinematic now. She was convinced that Joey from *Friends* was in *Arsenic and Old Lace*, despite it being made decades before Matt Le Blanc was born. My favourite responses to the evening's viewing were: "Who is that actor who always reminds me of Jack Lemmon?" and her genuine anger when Juliet Stevenson popped up. I never found out why. "She knows why," was all she gave me.

Sometimes I was unable to worry out the name of each actor she was thinking of on demand, even though some of the actors didn't appear on the screen, their memory was prompted by the appearance of somebody else. It was like playing a game of Guess Who twice removed. My inability to place the mystery person always disappointed her: "You used to be good at this!" she'd say, as though there were a point in time when I could gaze into her mind and map out her thought processes from no information.

And, of course, she was right. There was a time I could do exactly that.

My parents' deaths hit me unexpectedly hard. I became very depressed and briefly moved in with Silvia, whom I hadn't seen for years. I'm not sure whose idea it was, and I soon moved out again as we quickly realised it had been a mistake. But after a hot-housed month of intense scrutiny, I could accurately map out whole evenings of Silvia's idiosyncratic and active television watching.

Tonight's assertion had been Americans couldn't do collars.

"What do you mean Americans can't do collars?"

"Look," she said, as Jimmy Stewart put his foot up in *Rear Window*, "look at his collar. Rubbish."

"He's not meant to look smart. He's a grouchy, down-at-heel photographer with a broken leg!"

"No, they all look bad, all of them. It's the collars. Just the collars."

I knew what this was. These were the symptoms of loneliness. Silvia was always alone. Watching television was a bonding opportunity for her. The films were not entertainment in and of themselves, they were springboards to a larger narrative. They were a stepping-off point. They *included* me. My aunt knew something I was good at, perhaps the only thing I was good at—naming obscure actors—and she wanted me to impress her. When she recapped the start of the story over the middle of the story so ultimately, she had no idea what was going on at the end of the story, that didn't matter. That was not the point. She knew I would know. She knew I could read a film.

That night she slept upright on the sofa, her head thrown back as though seized with laughter. I removed her glasses. Her teeth had come loose, drawing in and out with each sonorous snore, peeping like a cat's tongue, so I picked them out, placing them beside her glasses on the coffee table. I fetched a blanket, draped it over her and continued to watch old films on her TV, drinking her wine in silence as I had done every Boxing Day for the past ten years. When I finally went to bed, I kissed her on the forehead. In our tiny family we only showed any affection when the other person was unconscious.

The fight has left her in the last couple of years. She's merely pass-remarkable now, no longer devastating. There were a few early jabs this afternoon, but for rest of the day she was almost companionable. It worried me. She wasn't herself.

In the morning, as always, she betrayed no hint of the previous night's excesses, being bright and neat with just the tiniest edge in her manner, as though expecting bad news.

"I'm going to go." I said.

"I expect you're busy." She knew I wasn't busy.

"Same time next year?" I said.

"If you like, if I'm still clinging to life."

"You're like lichen on a rock, Silvia. Nothing's going to scrape you off." We hugged, stiffly.

On returning home I took my jacket off, and there once again was the powdery outline of her face pressed onto my lapel. The ghost of a smile.

WILL ALEXANDER

NERVOUS ELECTRICAL COMPOUNDING

Say
the nerve ends glisten
as stark neuronal turquoise
not as nervous hatchery
but as evolutive emblem hatching via proto-memory
prior to the wastes of the Cambrian electrification
unleashing being
being mystery as the soilless body
reaching back to non-existent amplification compounded as proto-statistic that remains
uncountable
as hallucinatory proto-body
unleashing being as its own being
its channel alive as electrical compounding
as spurious trilogies
as spur to the unknown
as possible horseshoe crab
being curious electrical hatchery
before the drought of ideology as discipline
the latter we know as nerves according to civil compunction
not rival oblong statute
or claim as summoned ambrosia
being dazed human alacrity
yet I'm thinking of bursts as patterns
not in a prone or optical sense
but in the manner that starfish ignite their crescents as neon

Andrew McKeown

O Come, O Come

It was the night after Christmas. Judd was in the house alone, watching television in the dark. The gas fire breathed orange and blue.

First he heard a car—a deep, reverberating noise, like that of a taxi—the rattle of its diesel engine flattening out to a ticking-over sound as it came to a halt outside. Next came the sound of a vehicle door opening and through the yellow curtains he saw a light come on somewhere in the road.

There was a knock at the front door.

Judd got up, paused for a moment in silence then went into the hall. Here he switched on the light.

An unfamiliar silhouette stood out in the glass of the door. Opening this, his eyes focused slowly and with some difficulty on a woman his brother's age, standing in the porch. She had dark hair and wore a man's thick overcoat which she wrapped around her body in double-breasted fashion. She looked with familiarity at Judd and seemed sure of her purpose. Behind her in the taxi there was another woman looking down at something she held in her lap.

'Is he in?'

The woman spoke first with assurance.

Judd looked at her blankly.

Faltering, she looked back over her shoulder.

Judd saw her in profile and wondered if he did not know her. Just as he was going to say something she gathered herself, took an envelope out of her pocket and handed it to him:

'It's for your father. Make sure he gets it.'

She looked over her shoulder again and then once more at Judd:

'Well, I'll be seeing you.'

He watched her walk back to the taxi and get in, placing a hand on the thing the other woman was holding.

Judd shut the door and listened as the vehicle started off, slowing at the corner then accelerating again, up through the gears and disappearing out of earshot along the main road.

Christmas had started early in December, as usual.

At the hospital, the nurses had sellotaped red and green crêpe paper chains over the doors. Greetings cards filled the bedside tables. When Judd went to visit he counted the number his mother had received. *Season's Greetings* and *Noel, Noel* they proclaimed, their stars and angelic hosts shedding a fine dust of glitter come unstuck from its glue.

'Father Waring's coming to give Holy Communion on Christmas morning.'

Judd's mother spoke with enthusiasm.

Vietcong. Judd heard himself silently repeat the priest's little joke, calling to the altar boys for them to line up in the sacristy before Mass. Waring's visit reminded Judd that he too would have to come to the hospital on Christmas day, maybe even spend the afternoon there.

'Nice of him to come just for me.'

His mother smiled, acknowledging a favour. Judd smiled back.

His mother had been in hospital for six months. There was no talk of whether she might come home again. The MS that had been diagnosed soon after Judd was born now left her immobile up to the neck.

Judd's mother continued:

'Have you got the tree up yet?'

At the house, the Christmas tree stood as usual in the alcove next to the television. Every year Judd carefully unfolded and arranged its coathanger arms, stretching over them gold and silver trains of tinsel, hanging them with coloured glass balls, so as to look like Christmas in the department stores.

Underneath the tree there were presents already waiting—the gift-wrapped toiletry set for his mother, for example, still redolent of the gust of fragrant well-being that had greeted Judd as he entered the chemist's the day he bought the package.

And the skateboard he was to receive, wrapped by his own hand. Sometimes he would pick up the parcel and admire it. Sometimes he undid the wrapper and skated round the room.

'California style,' he would say to himself aloud, half joking, flicking a ball on the Christmas tree as he rolled past, slowly over the carpet.

As Christmas approached there was the customary talk of snow in the newspapers. Seasonal films filled up the TV programmes. There was a concert at school.

In that final week Judd's brother went out every night.

Before leaving he would play his records in the back room and come to dance in the kitchen, leaving the black and white linoleum tiles scored with little whirls. Judd watched him through the serving hatch that connected the two rooms and thought of his brother later going between pubs with his friends. How exciting their world seemed, Judd thought. What noisy exchanges they must have!

Judd was usually in bed when his brother came back. Once earlier that year, during another period of intense socialising that had marked his brother's 18th birthday, Judd had awoken in the night and noticed the bed opposite his own was empty. Sensing something unusual in the house he went downstairs and pushed open the living room door.

His brother was stretched out on the carpet. Next to him there was a woman, her back to the door. She was half undressed and was sitting on the floor, propped against the armchair, her leg drawn up underneath her. Sections of pale skin stood out against the brown carpet.

There was a moment's stillness. Then she moved her head to the side and Judd saw her in profile, looking at his brother lying prostrate on his back like one of those men in Flemish harvest paintings. She turned away again. Judd closed the door and went back to bed.

Finally Christmas morning came and, just as the house was beginning to wake, it started to snow.

'The papers were right.'

His father was calling from downstairs.

Judd jumped from his bed. Through his window he saw the snow banked up against the garden walls, settling on the cars and hedges. A woman walked past along the pavement, her footfalls landing silently as the snow accumulated. Beyond the houses, toward the horizon of trees and pylons, a white envelope of snow was forming.

His father's voice came again:

'Will you collect the presents, Judd? The bus for the hospital leaves in thirty minutes.'

When it was time they set off into the avenue, Judd, his father and his brother walking without speaking, Judd carrying the presents in a plastic bag. As they came on to the main road a solitary car approached, its muffled presence adhering uncertainly to the white surface.

Fare Stage. Judd noted the familiar, half-comprehended sign at the bus stop then turned his gaze to follow the sweep of the snow.

Presently the bus emerged out of the grainy distance, its diesel-engine hum preceding a brightly-lit array of windows carried on broad, black tyres rolling gently over the white road, catching chunks of snow in their tread then letting them fall, like cake crumbling.

At the hospital the ward was over-warm, as usual. Another family were standing around a bed to the left, talking quietly. There were no other visitors. Some beds had curtains drawn around them. His mother's head was turned toward the door as they entered.

At the far end of the long room a door opened on to the TV lounge. Inside there were patients slumped in heavy, vinyl-covered armchairs mounted on thick rubber wheels, now parked in a semi-circle in front a screen hidden from Judd's view behind a door. He could see the flickering light move across their forms, the distended silhouettes of the patients cast up on the ceiling. He knew the empty expressions of their faces, the air of hospital meals and cleaning products they carried with them. Christmas, Judd thought. This wasn't his idea of Christmas.

'Shall we bring your meal over to you here?'

One of the nurses had come to the bed.

'So you can all eat together?'

Judd's parents smiled and it was quietly agreed.

'Father Waring was here this morning,' his mother began. 'Just the two of us and the blind woman from the next ward. All Protestants here, I suppose.'

Judd's father was smiling.

'He came to have a cigarette with me afterwards. Apparently the crib at church was vandalised last night.'

As she spoke the garden shed they put up outside church every year stood out in Judd's mind—its almost-lifesize figures dressed in Bible outfits, some standing, some kneeling, with the donkey and the sheep, all bowing their heads toward the vacant manger.

'He'd just gone to put the baby Jesus in place for midnight Mass,' his mother's voice continued.

At that moment the roar of a motorcycle from the TV room caught Judd's ear. He looked round. There were German voices, too, shouting from beyond the wheelie armchairs, and more motorbikes. And then music playing.

The Great Escape, Judd said to himself.

'Somebody had sprayed *Blackpool FC* on the perspex window. The lock was broken and the shepherds were holding cans of beer, with lipstick smeared all around their mouths.'

The noise of the motorbikes and the music rose to a pitch, culminating in a volley of machine gun fire. Judd could see Steve McQueen caught in the barbed wire:

'*Los aufstehen.*'

'And someone had put . . .'

His mother's voice cut out as the German guard gave another order:

'*Hände hoch!*'

'. . . in the manger.'

As they tutted—Judd's parents seemed to find the story of the crib a convenient subject for dismay—one of the television group suddenly began shouting, setting off an unintelligible commotion. A nurse briskly intervened, then reappeared in the ward, went directly to a low cupboard where she collected towels and a flat, stainless steel pan and went back into the TV room.

While his parents continued to discuss the Christmas crib and as the jumble of cinema and patients' confusion continued to spill out of the TV lounge, Judd's mind focused unexpectedly, with no animosity or resentment, on a thought that had never occurred to him before:

'What have I to do with this place?'

The ring of chairs in the TV lounge was disarrayed. One of the patients was standing now, her hospital shift untied at the back and raised above her waist. The woman was holding a tube, trying to insert it back into her abdomen but not succeeding.

'Judd, what about the presents?'

His father's voice came to him suddenly, out of nothing.

Judd gathered himself, reached for the bag and set the gifts on the bed. In turn they opened each package, placing them next to her: a scarf from Marks and Spencer's, a box of Milk Tray chocolates and the presentation set of Tweed perfume.

'Thank you,' she said, looking across the gifts.

Judd looked again at his mother in the bed and regretted the thought he had had. It was not her fault. He wanted to say he was sorry. At times he imagined there was some huge mistake or some all-powerful remedy. Like the perfume he had brought her, like Christmas.

Someone in the TV room had started to whistle the film's closing theme tune.

Around the bed they talked about the snow and the bus ride into town and what was on television later that day.

Elsewhere in the hospital nurses were taking party crackers out of large cardboard boxes, people in the kitchens were getting meals ready on formica trays.

It was Christmas.

When the road was silent again Judd went into the kitchen and put the kettle on. His mind was uneasy and he thought again about the face in profile.

When the water came to the boil he pressed the back of the letter against the steam coming out of the spout and worked the envelope open. There was a handwritten sheet of paper inside, with a date and the words, *La Sagesse, North Shore*, printed in cursive type in the top right-hand corner.

To whom it may concern, the note began. *I have just given birth to a baby boy. I am calling him after your son whose the father.* Judd paused and re-read whose the father and questioned if this was the right grammar. *I hope he gets to meet his grandad soon. Yours sincerely.*

'*Sincerely*, for someone you know,' Judd remembered from school.

The paper was signed at the bottom but it was hard to read: *Angela* something or other, it read. *PS* it concluded, *Happy Christmas.*

Judd put the note back in the envelope and sealed it again, smoothed it down with the heel of his hand and put it on the meter cupboard where other letters were kept.

Later that night from his bed Judd heard his brother and his dad come home. The sounds of the kettle being filled and the television coming to life rose through the house.

Unable to put the letter out of his thoughts Judd got up and went quietly on to the landing. A light came on in the hall. From his hidden vantage, Judd saw a hand reach for the envelope then watched as another hand joined it, turned the note around and back again and around once more then worked a thumb under its flap. The stairwell filled for an instant with the tiny rasp of the paper inside being withdrawn.

Then there was nothing. The light in the hall went out.

Judd returned to his bedroom and drew back the curtain. Sitting on the edge of his bed, watching the black rectangle of his window, he waited.

Linda Mannheim

At Liberty

Down by the Murrumbidgee River, David eases his truck onto the dirt road, and shines his headlights onto the shadowed path. He's showing me where I can go running in the morning. The lights glint off the inky shimmering water. We drive through an underpass and the headlights expose murals painted onto the cement. Aborigine art, David tells me proudly. I should look for them when I come back in the morning.

David was waiting at the petrol station when the bus dropped me off. I'd had a feeling he would be here, though we hadn't made plans to meet until the next morning. He was concerned about me finding my way from the bus drop off to the B&B, so he stood outside the convenience store waiting for me to appear. And I knew immediately when I looked over that he was David Houston, president of the Dunera Museum at Hay, lifelong resident of Hay, New South Wales.

David was a six-year-old boy when the men from the Dunera disembarked from the train and walked to the newly constructed internment camp with its three barbed wire fences and four guard towers. The big children were brought there by their schools, but David came on his own with another boy and the people of the town all watched as the men from the Dunera were led from the train to the camp. David remembers: The men wore odd woollen overcoats, city hats, European clothes.

My father was one of those men, one of the refugees from Germany and Austria rounded up in England in 1940, declared an 'enemy alien', and shipped to Australia after initial internment on an unfinished housing estate in Liverpool and after that on the Isle of Man. He would have been one of the youngest men transported to Australia, sent on the HMT Dunera, emerging after weeks below deck, imprisoned on an overcrowded ship, then sent on a guarded train to Hay.

What do you remember about it? I ask David.

All the trains, he says. Hay was a small town. He'd never seen so many trains at once.

Hay was the perfect place for an internment camp, David explains. Far from the coast, far from everything—to discourage escape attempts. But near a rail line, and near farmland so that food for the two thousand men could be supplied. The acquisition of the land, the construction of the internment camp—it all happened quickly. You don't usually see government move that quickly, he reflects.

Were people here upset that Hay was chosen for the camp? Did they think: Not in my back yard?

They were happy for the work, David answers, happy for the business. The camp needed food, clothing, blankets. The guards wanted somewhere to go drink. The town's population doubled.

I've come to Australia to document my father's story, try to find the pieces of his history that had fallen away, try to fathom someone who was frequently misunderstood, who I believed I'd misunderstood. David was used to children of former prisoners showing up with similar missions: to see this place that their fathers spoke of so much, to stand in a place that listeners would later say couldn't have existed. Because how could you explain Britain imprisoning Second World War refugees when it was supposed to have been the place that welcomed people fleeing? How could you explain the need they had to send those refugees someplace so far away from the part of the world where they'd lived up until then?

My father spoke about Australia constantly when I was growing up, remembered it with a weird mixture of resentment and ardour. He fell in love with the country where he was imprisoned, nurtured his memories of it during all the years after the war, after he settled and had a family in a rundown section of New York City. Australia was the place that was unlike anyplace else, with kangaroos and Southern Hemisphere constellations, unstoppable wind and crazy deserts.

The day the men from the Dunera arrived, there was a dust storm in Hay. This happened regularly there—40 degree heat, and a billowing cloud of dust booms: dust in the air, in the men's mouths, on their eyelids. There was always dust everywhere. The men from the Dunera were to be sent to a different camp, a new one in Tatura where the climate was "more suitable for Europeans." This was 1941; the Italians came to Hay when the men from the Dunera moved on. David could hear them singing sometimes. They were put to work hauling wood. The local girls thought the Italians were all Valentino. There were Japanese prisoners later on too.

The former internment camp towns—Hay, Tatura, Orange—all have museum exhibits dedicated to the history of those camps, have become sites of pilgrimage for those who know about the use of these isolated places, or are sites of curiosity for those driving across sparsely populated territory. The dark night skies blaze with stars in these quiet places. When David takes me to visit local people or brings me to the restaurant where he's a regular, it's like being in any small forgotten place where a newcomer inspires interest.

Who's this? someone asks, coming over to a table set with paper placements and sweating water glasses.

The daughter of one of the Dunera men, David answers. She's a writer from London. I'm working on a book, I add. I'm here to do to research.

On the main road, we drive slowly down the single road banked with motels, with brightly lit restaurants for travellers on their way to Sydney or Adelaide.

David's father was a communist, a principled man, David remembers. He read left-wing pa-

pers. He knew the prisoners coming weren't Nazi. They were Jews and there wasn't any reason to b afraid of them, he told David.

Down by the Murrumbidgee River, everyon used to go swim. There was a girl who drowne there. They had to get one of the Japanese pea divers out of the internment camp and ask him t retrieve her body, David explains. The diver didn want to touch her when he saw her golden hai wavering in the water, furling and unfurling wit the current.

We drive up the dirt road, back toward the cen tre of town. But there's a cop car on the side of th path, and David, as instructed, pulls over. A youn cop comes over to the driver's door; David rolls hi window down. He hands over his license and th cop waves a plastic wand in front of David; he ask David to say his name into it. David does. The co looks at the wand and confirms that David is n drunk. He hands back David's license and thank us for our cooperation.

It's the first time I have ever interacted with cop in this country. They remind me so much of Ameri can cops that, hearing them, I felt disoriented. Cop with funny accents, I thought. And these, I ob served, the ones we dealt with here—they didn quite have the swagger American police can hav when they pull you over. No sunglasses, no slic hips, no sir and no ma'am and no boy.

They weren't bad, David explains, starting th truck again. They can be a lot worse than that. Bu it's helpful to be eighty years old in this kind of sit uation, he adds. They were looking for drugs. Ha is the stopping off point between Sydney and Ade laide now, and unfortunately a good place to traf fic. People have to lock their cars now, lock th doors of their houses, mind themselves.

Heroin? I guess.

And ice, David informs.

Down by the Murrumbidgee River, at the end o the dusty main street, past the restaurant where amples of locally grown wool and cotton sit in little piles on display, there's a museum in the disused train station, and outside it a search light just like the one they used to have at the internment camp. They switch it on at 6:30 in the evening so you can see the searchlight beam up, whiten the dark dark sky. And the museum can be seen from far away—from the elevated highway over there, and from the motels where the travellers to Adelaide and Sydney stay over. They can find out about the prisoners who were once held here—the civilians who were interned, and the prisoners of war.

I imagine being one of those travellers: taking a break from a long drive, from the hum drum of the highway. I imagine getting out of the car, smoothing my clothes, rolling back my shoulders and telling my travel companion that it's good to be out of the car. I imagine going to the restaurant and telling the waitress where I've come from and where I'm going. And I imagine having no relationship to this place. So that when the searchlight beams up, I can turn my head to the sky and make a stupid joke. And when I walk into the museum, every item will be a curiosity to me, something I find interesting because I never knew such things might exist. And when I get where I'm going, I might mention this place and I might not.

And I'll hear about the children of the former detainees who come here, and I'll wonder: What's that like? Do they come here looking for something their fathers couldn't reveal? Did their fathers, unable to explain why they were interned, feel forever tinged by guilt after they were here? And do those children whose fathers were interned here try to imagine themselves inside the camp, and then stop imagining it?

Or do they walk, like I do, all over the town, catch rides with kind hosts to places their fathers could never see when they were here, think: It is good to be here and see what there was and good to be at liberty.

Maureen Owen

Three Poems

Recipe

For Kyran

I washed folded wrapped
the aprons   the puffy white baker's cap
you a child perched   on a
kitchen chair stirring wore
shipping them to you
for your own   young

Wabi-sabi

Shirley's nickname was Shirt
Shirt and Ray   they had 10 kids or 11
and lived   in the San Pedro docks   housing
a big padlock with chain encircled
their refrigerator door   so all the food wouldn't
get eaten   Frances   their eldest daughter
tall and blond and so beautiful   I was ten   and she was about
sixteen I guess   Frances leaned out the window on a summer night   laughing
joking in a white Spanish embroidered blouse   passage to a foreign shore
I wanted to be like her   her smoky sweet voice
full of fun teasing brothers   making all the cousins laugh
including my brothers and I   recent cousins   our step dad Shirt's baby brother
when we stayed over   all us extra cousins piled into one big bed   about 7 or 8 of us
older kids telling scary stories to the younger   diving in and out of sheets and covers
on a visit their dog parenting puppies   Shirt gave us one   liver-colored spots   floppy ears
and a peachy nose   We named him Lucky

NEITHER DOZY MOTHS   NOR   THEIR GAUZY SWARMS
PENUMBRA   BUNDLING THRU SHADOW

"Do you see it flying up there   near the ceiling?"
"No, what is it?"
"the night bird   up in the corner   near the ceiling ..."

Two earrings dangle from a fork prong
fussy occupation   but up close
volant   somewhere above her bed

highlights vary   unstable mishmash
no surface flat enough   off-kilter shadow
bending voices   ignoring

what seethes within that plumage
sucks from the room   all oxygen
vegetation thick as thunder   knots between us
into some   exotic vacuum

Kurt Luchs

Choose a Star: David Ignatow and the Power of Plain Speaking

There are writers we love as readers, for the enjoyment they give us and their angle on the human experience; and there are writers we love as writers, for what they can teach us about our craft. Sometimes a writer is both things to us, but not always. While I enjoy T.S. Eliot and Ezra Pound, in moderation, for various reasons that don't bear going into here, they could never serve as models for me to follow, in art or (heaven help me) in life.

Ever since I first encountered David Ignatow's poetry in the early Seventies, I have taken much from it as a reader and as a writer. He could be described as the love child of Walt Whitman and William Carlos Williams, with, as Robert Bly observed, a little Hemingway thrown in. His poems are almost always plain and unassuming, usually free verse, occasionally prose poems, yet they pack a powerful sucker punch that sneaks up on you. This is all the more remarkable in that, as James Dickey wrote in an early review, "Ignatow does almost completely without the traditional skills of English versification." In the right hands, apparently, no technique is also a technique.

The poem I want to discuss here, "For My Daughter," is quite short, only 15 lines, three simple sentences, two stanzas. It dates from the Sixties and did not find its way into a book until Ignatow's first collected volume, *Poems 1934–1969* (Wesleyan 1970). Judging by how many web sites it appears

on today, it must be one of his best-loved works. It begins:

> When I die choose a star
> and name it after me
> that you may know
> I have not abandoned
> or forgotten you.

Official practice would be to put commas after "die" and "me." The more sensible practice adopted by Ignatow, regardless of rules, is to avoid punctuation except where the lack of it would leave the passage less clear. Poets should trust their instincts and the intelligence of their readers. His line breaks in this sentence do the work of punctuation, and the run-on first line has the effect of leaping past the idea of his mortality right into how his daughter can begin to handle it. We infer that, just as he is now introducing her to death, he once introduced her to stargazing, an age-old father-daughter pastime. Note how quickly and effortlessly he has made the personal universal. What father has not wondered how to have this conversation with his children? And who else but Ignatow would be so disarmingly direct yet gentle?

The second sentence amplifies and inverts this thought: "You were such a star to me, / following you through birth / and childhood, my hand / in your hand." Did you catch that? He's not holding her hand in his, he's letting her hold his hand in hers, a subtle but meaningful difference, and part of the quiet brilliance of this poem. It is the natural order of things for the caregiver to become the one needing care, and for the child to become the parent. Natural or not, though, it is a painful reality that is difficult to face, and from the beginning he intends to help his daughter do that.

The third and final sentence also functions as the second stanza. It starts by repeating the first two lines of the poem, breaking them a little differently so that the whole stanza has some of the run-on feeling of the first line, for heightened anticipation. By the time we get to the last four lines we are nearly ready for the emotional weight that the poem has accumulated:

> ...so that I may shine
> down on you, until you join
> me in darkness and silence
> together.

And that, ladies and gentlemen, is how you talk to your daughter about death, yours and hers and everyone's. Small wonder that James Wright titled his essay about Ignatow "A Plain Brave Music" (see Wright's *Collected Prose*, The University of Michigan Press 1983).

David Ignatow was born in 1914, the same yea as another fine American poet, Randall Jarrell, bu outlived his contemporary by 32 years, producin several dozen books of verse. Jarrell died in 196! and only four years later his *Complete Poems* was i print. I can hardly believe that Ignatow died i 1997, almost a quarter of a century ago, and we ar still waiting for his *Complete Poems*. I would make special plea to Wesleyan University Press, whic holds the rights to many of his books, and to the Li brary of America, which specializes in suc projects, to put all of Ignatow's work within eas reach of poetry lovers in his country. It is not to much to ask for this most American of poets.

KURT LUCHS

FOR MY DAUGHTERS

(after "For My Daughter" by David Ignatow)

When you scatter my ashes in Northside Park
many years from now (I hope,
though we have no say in these things),
let the wind take them and become
my voice, invisible, a wordless song
known only by its singular note
and its ability to make leaves and branches
dance like little green puppets
for your pleasure and amusement.
After the leaves have stilled and hushed,
the wind that is me will have moved
into the echo chamber of memory
where endings try so hard not to end.
Yet every song must have an ending.
I thought I knew what joy was
before you came to me. I doubt I will know
what grief is until I must say goodbye.
I would rather let the wind say it for me,
and the long brown grasses on the shore
of the pond where we looked for turtles together,
and the water rippling with tiny waves
carried beyond themselves
into the darkening dusk.

Robert Musil

Aphorisms

From *Robert Musil: Literature and Politics*,
translated by Genese Grill
(Contra Mundum, 2022)

*G*leichschaltung. Another measure of the strangeness of what is happening today with the German spirit is that a word has come into usage for a large part of these happenings, a word that presents the native speaker with no less difficulty than it does a foreigner. "Schalten," the action word at its foundation, belongs to the older history of the German language and had possessed in the present day only a weakened life, so that there were indeed many derivations of it in use, while it itself was somewhat petrified and only used in specific combinations. So one can say, for example, that someone *schaltet frei* (disconnects or isolates) from something, but the simple sentence one *schaltet* no longer carries a complete meaning. On the whole, the word is most often seen in the formula "schalten und walten," which means something to the effect of 'to manage and to have a free hand,' but which is spun with a bit of poetical moss. One grasps that there is some Romanticism behind the idea of using the word *schalten*. Its original meaning signifies to push, tow, set in motion, force.

This Romantic word has the most modern of children. A *Schalter* is something at the train station, namely a 'ticket office,' and something having to do with electrical room lighting signifies a little window that one can push open and closed, but also there is, in an electric power station, something called a large "Schalt-bord."

According to *Der Tag* of December 24th 1935 the "National Socialist Party Correspondent" writes: "The judgment in the Reichstag arson trial, whereby Torgler and the three Bulgarians were set free on legal technicalities, is, according to the people's feeling for justice, a flat-out false judgment. If the judgment had been delivered in accordance with the true justice which should again be valued in Germany, it would have been formulated differently. The entire basis and conducting of the trial, which was witnessed by the whole *Volk* with growing dissatisfaction, would, however, have had to have been different." These "technicalities" consisted of the fact that the state court of law could not be convinced that the grounds of the charges were sufficient.

Every feeling, every uninhibited person is radical. A component of the law arises here: the law must also protect the law-breaker! Otherwise a lie will be punished by the death penalty. See for example the condoning of castration for exhibitionists (*Der Tag* December 24, 1935) put at the discretion of the judge.

On the other hand: legal punishment is really a tolerating of the crime; this has its price. One must "pursue the crime"; this is what the strong state demands; utilize every means until it is exterminated. (And the argument about whether the prohibitive effect increases or does not increase along with the cruelty of the punishment?)

The danger of the writer

[. . .]

Gleichschaltung

1) The word

It marks the strangeness (it will be difficult for foreigners to understand it) of what is happening today in Germany, that this word *Gleichschaltung*, which plays such a large role in it, cannot be directly translated into other languages. This word was suddenly there one day out of nowhere for the not-yet-National Socialist Germans. Lamps, machines are *gleichgeschaltet* [switched into conformity]—and Germans. Difference between norms and similarities. It has active and passive meanings in psychiatry. Levers and similar mechanisms, electric currents *ein-* und *ausschalten* [switch on and off]. *Schaltwerk* [control unit]. *Schalthebel* [switching lever]. In general: *Gleichstrom* (co- or parallel current): a current whose direction remains the same. There is a *Batterieschaltung* [accumulator switch] for galvanic elements, next to and following one another. One speaks of (different) modes of *Schaltung* in dynamo machines. Likewise, in an electrical lighting system.

Schalten, Middle High German. To push, tow (esp. a ship), into movement, to force. In New High German becomes = to steer; Old High German *scaltan* = to push, New High German *Schalter* = sliding sash [window] from Middle High German *schalter* (*schelter*) = [a] bolt. *Schaltjahr* [leap year] already in old high German because of the day that is 'shoved in' (To shove is also a basic meaning of *schalten*). *Walten* really means to be strong, see *Gewalt* [violence].

Incorporating of the *Verwalten* [powers/administration]. Permeation with National Socialist spirit and National Socialist form. Permeation with a spirit (and therein lies the difference from norms).

> The writer speaks: I was never party. I was always on my own. I have done my duty. But now they want to keep me from doing it. This is why I am here.

Goebbels: The intellect can never be creative, doesn't produce anything new. Understanding sees everything from two sides. Possible continuation: Reason and emotion in politics. Discipline [. . .] also belongs here, in part retort too. That they can even speak of a National Socialist *Weltanschauung*. (Group opinion would be better!)

On the whole: [. . .] philosophical stringency, philosophical pathos (Nietzsche) fail! I am not a philosopher; I am a creative writer.

Completion [*Ausführung*] speaks against the philosophy of power. All completion speaks against that which remains to be completed. Song of praise for Democracy *à la* Kakania.

Propaganda for Germany, but not possible in Germany. Action and thought. Since Goethe.

Philosophy of power is a partial solution. Include knowledge of it, but don't bring it into being.

'The land without No. The *Volk* where on doesn't say No. Question: What has to happen i the spiritual person affirms everything an hands on everything that comes from above' What does 'above' mean? Random personal ex pressions and inclinations of the *Führer*? Propa ganda minister.

Spirit of the party, of the Combat League[s], etc Staid institutions.

While observing a large fat man with a briefcase in the trolley, 6 o'clock in the evening: he is coming from school or from the office. He doesn't want to tire himself anymore. National Socialism gives him the feeling that something is happening and that it is well on its way; Germany is in strong hands, while he deservedly rests. That is really much more natural than to take up the newspaper, to study battles of opinions and suchlike. Parliamentarianism, with its journalism etc., wanted to be Athenian but has really only managed to achieve a caricature.

The inexpressible literary content of a painting; I wanted to reduce the image's effect to that, to raise the image to honor again. But can there be something inexpressible = literary? *Contradictio in adjecto?* It is the lyrical. Pictures of battles, genre scenes have a rational content. One can only write a poem or make circumscriptions about the dying dueler. That's also the source of the awkward character of poems set to music; there are two forms: poems can, at best, only be set to music in a half-dismantled condition.

Arithmetical simile: human unity and cooperation has two forms: one reduces everything to its smallest common multiple or searches for the greatest common denominator. I strive for the former; the latter has already been attempted by the democratic newspapers when they orient their novel sections toward the stupidest reader. One can also say: make a whole out of the people, possibly of the nation, or give it a feeling, an idea.

Jake Goldsmith

On CF and Possibility

Science-fiction writers have been known to default to using cystic fibrosis as an example of a disease that will simply be eradicated by gene modification. This is due to a wider perception of what the illness is, and also to popular perceptions of the advancement of genetics research, and our knowledge and control over genetics. This includes the optimistic, even transhuman ideas that feature the overcoming, through knowledge, of nature—and scientific, or technological, utopianism, in a broader sense. Even our fundamental reckoning with nature, with death, and of escaping it. Big things we are playing with here.

Cystic Fibrosis research has seen the development of a newer generation of drugs, such as Kaftrio and others, with a lot of hope and investment placed in them that they may essentially eradicate many, if not all, of the problems people with CF will face—this being a step towards further exciting research.

This is only partly true, and we have to be blunt here. It also represents in a greater sense a fundamentally misguided optimism about human control and capability, including the idea of the eventual eradication of all disease and disability.

To put it simply, this is hubris.

More specifically, these newer drugs have been and can be of some benefit to those with more common CF mutations, and you may well know people who have seen some great improvements. What is neglected are those for whom these drugs are not even an option to begin with due to the incompatibility of their mutations. CF can be caused by thousands of different mutations in millions of different permutations, some of them utterly unique. Again, more broadly, despite the temptation to believe otherwise, we do not understand as much about genetics as we think, and much of it remains nebulous. Neurology, psychiatry, genetics—these are all more complex fields of medicine than we admit. They will remain less understood by us than we would like, even with growing technological advancements, and they are definitely not well-conceived by hubristic quack and woo understandings of either the human body or of life generally.

You may point to the more optimistic stories and begrudge my pessimism, but here's the thing: you fucking always point to the optimistic stories. Less than glowing accounts frighten and discomfort you, so that you constantly remind us of good news and vague hopes. But you appear less concerned with my own discomfort and terror—a terror far more acute than your outside view because I'm the one who will actually face these choices, the pain, and all these contentions being thought about neurotically and every day. You aren't in my body. You go to work and interact with conventional society while I sit (most of the time) indoors with far less to distract me—barely coping with my bodily functions and thinking about my expiration date. Forgive me if tales of success and sugarcoating don't bring me joy. They're distant. I prefer my hard truth to your fretting over what's happening to me and what is possible for me. I'm the one experiencing this. You think you're uncomfortable or scared, seeing me as some grim example or an unsettling reminder of grave things, but I'm the one actually having to live this. I am consumed by righteous indignation—born, as I see it, into a cruel world that was immediately unjust to me, unjust in volumes to so many others, with no convincing metaphysical or cosmological justification for any of it at all, with only mundane things being of any possible comfort: friends and family offering some solace. I'd be animated and angry if I wasn't so absolutely drained of fortitude.

I'm happier and more good-humoured in other writing.

And no, you don't think about life and death like this—not habitually. Death may be real to you but it is also much more distant; it is faraway or accidental, you are young, and not many actually live life unto death, in a consistent sense at least. You can afford not to think about it given that it is far less pressing. God, I have written all this shit before! If you don't want to get it then you won't. It's a matter of your life and view on things being comprised of such different concerns. You aren't ill!

I wrote a whole fucking book about this with the perverse intention of it standing as a testament to who I am and what I believe—that could be read as an easy biographical introduction to me. It details a phenomenology of illness and a life defined through the lens of chronic illness. I took the title of the book (*Neither Weak Nor Obtuse*) from a phrase in a letter Boris Pasternak sent to Albert Camus, regarding sensualism as our only recourse in life—in that such may be the case, but if it is utterly naked (i.e. unfettered and extreme), and holds similar conceits to supernatural or theological salvation, then it becomes weak and obtuse. Struggling with this brand of materialism without the availability of convincing spiritual or metaphysical avenues is a major part of this phenomenology.

Returning to the fabled wonder drugs (as they're described): for those who are genetically eligible to take these newer drugs, they can come with numerous side effects and intolerances (sickness, mood swings, a long list of other complications) that may make their use impossible. Beyond 'miracle drugs', transplantation and other 'fixes' for the symptoms of CF are not so amazing either. Transplantation can only, commonly, offer a few more years if successful, if that, and otherwise comes with multiple recurrent risks such as organ rejection. Or it may just not work at all. And for all the healthy, non-disabled people out there who can idly and blithely say things, as you always do: the world is much more complicated than you think, and this is not your choice.

I want to be allowed to be angry. When I am stoical or childishly funny, remaining stern and academic or making jokes at everything and not taking much seriously, I am better tolerated. I use humour and have a playful sense of childishness. I don't think I'm very funny in my writing, because I only write about intimate things—which can of course be funny, but I mostly do so very seriously. I express love and adoration and gratitude. For once I want to be absolutely enraged and not feel regretful about it afterwards. I feel an ambivalence towards

prolonging my life if it will be too painful. I valu comfort more highly. I want quiet. The world is ur just and I hate it, yet I have little hope in correctin it. I just want to relax in the garden.

Whether people think they are fonder of scien tific understanding or have stock in other hopes, trend they share is a massive over-estimation c human possibility and progress, as well as a per ception that disability and ill-health are fixable, c eventually fixable, phenomena we can compre hensively grapple and come to terms with Bluntly, disability is much more complex tha this. Illness is far more complicated and bemus ing than you ever think it is. And while it is cer tain that we will see medical advancements, th reach and potential of these need to be mor truthfully considered. For far too many these pre sumed hopes are remote, or simply ableist non sense. Enthused, toxic optimism from non-dis abled voices about 'cures' and fixes (especiall considering many different disabilities or healt concerns) is insulting, or even flagrant eugenicis evil. Cystic Fibrosis is a far different question from Deafness, or Down syndrome—obviously. If I ex pand on that more I may as well write volumes, s I will leave that to others. It's not in my curren scope to talk about all the variances and politics c disability, despite my wide digressions here. Ther are far more political barriers to disability justic than are considered, and frankly most have n idea, much of the time, about these different di mensions and what lives people live: with wha they have to face each day and contend with so reg ularly.

There is a constant condescension and a stoc ignorance regarding ill health. Even a global pan demic hasn't stopped people living as callously a they want, and the whole history of life-changin pandemics (this was never unprecedented) tha have caused such massive change throughout al of history—more so than any war or political up set—remains ubiquitously ignored or unknown It's unsurprising that hubris and ignorance re main so established.

So yes, I have been doing okay recently.

R.S. Mengert

Two Poems

Ghazal of Petition

I drink to be my father—the Kandinsky of calculus, abstractor
of abstractions. The next best thing to death is dreamless sleep.

This drinking is a type of combat: beat your dreams back
until they look like someone else's and leave you alone.

Head down on a Vegas bar, cigarettes and wallet in front of me, proof
of guardian angels. Or fresh meat. My dreams walk home to sleep it off.

A green-faced man of God reads Kant over a fifth of rubbing alcohol.
He passes out, dreams of car-sized cockroaches. Which is better?

I walked among the wakeful. I listened to their dreams. Their lies. Drink
to the certainty that they did not know me. Not a one.

Tell me how you do it, Hafez, how you navigate this nightmare
of their drunken universe while drunk with love. I am awake, and sober.

Carnival of Theodicy

It makes one like me tired
of the light
and all I can do is laugh and don my best black suit
to carry my remains as I die daily

into the everlasting sunlight of the day.
I am my constant pallbearer,
the ever-ready stiff who walks
through hazy funerals of afternoons.

I hold my remnants high, coffined
in a box of black canvas stretched
over plywood boards, and lead the march
that never makes it to my longed-for grave.

Office managers and priests, ex-lovers,
coworkers and schoolmates, dance
as they follow my parade with disapproving faces
in their sequined gowns and glittering top hats.

I alone hold up the coffin box.

A boy I hated in the 6th grade
offers to help, but I refuse
his company. I alone
must hold the box.

The office manager
who always hated me
stands off to the side
and laughs.

A New Orleans brass band escorts us.

Father O'Leary suggests they play *Requiem Aeternam*
or maybe "Whiskey in the Jar," but
a medley of pop hits from the 1980s
blasts from speakers mounted on the traffic lights

and lamp posts, the crumbling casino signs
of Old Downtown.
The rusty speakers blast
my funeral procession dirge:

rain keeps falling,
rain keeps falling,
down, down…

But it never rains.
Rain never cools

the endless sunlight of my daily funeral.
It makes one like me tired
of the light
as I die daily. The sun glows

sickly yellow, hot though dying
without end, like the flickering glare
of the old electric lamp that used to
burn me as I trembled

in my gray-walled room at night
alone,
back when I could stay inside,
when I could find a night,

a naught, a place to hide from day
where light was light and black was black
and I could hope to die
for good.

LJ Pemberton

Triangles Are Not Circles

I am going to tell you a story (a story has a beginning, a middle, and an end). The beginning: this, here, hi, I am telling you a story (a story has characters who do things). A character: Ed, yes let's call him Ed. Character two: let's say James. James is also a man. (I didn't tell you that Ed was a man, but you knew he was a man because I called him a him.) Character three—because there are more than two characters, of course—is Kate. Kate with a k. Kate with a k who is a woman (when she was a child she was identified as female and when she grew up she identified as a woman and so she didn't have to change her name). Kate, our culture says, is unambiguously female (unlike Chris or Alex or sometimes Leslie or Ryan or George). Three characters then, that you now know: Ed, James, and Kate.

There are more characters, but we will meet them later.

I am going to tell you a story (a story has a plot). A plot should be able to be stated quickly so that book publishers and movie executives will be interested without having to pay too much attention. A plot can be stated like this: a Marine veteran suddenly finds himself the leader of a small battalion of teenage boys and girls when their youth group encounters drug smugglers deep in the jungle of Costa Rica during a mission trip far from home. That is not the plot of this story, although it's the sort of action-packed colonial bullshit that Hollywood really goes for.

A plot can make you feel feelings: intrigue, boredom, sadness, happiness, etc. A plot can be called the spine of a story. Some writers and agents and publishers talk about fleshing out a plot or fleshing out a story or putting the skin on as though stories are people that are made fully grown by starting with a skeleton and then adding muscles and organs and finally skin and breath. I am glad people are not made that way. To be honest, I don't think stories should be made that way either.

I am going to tell you a story. This story is about love. Most stories are about love even if they are about violence. Violence is a form of love. I am not excusing violence by calling it love. I am using metaphorical language. Life as blood. Feeling as heart. Bleeding as breathing. Violence as love. Kate has a wish about love. She wishes she could stop thinking about James. She wishes that she could turn her mind back into itself. Like she could live her life for only herself instead of pausing at the checkout counter and considering whether she should buy chocolate for James or checking her phone for a message from him or considering what he might say about that H&M advertisement at the bus stop. She wishes she could move through the world and not wonder what he is thinking or whether he is thinking of their day or her because she knows (she suspects) that he is not.

Kate has a wish about love because she did not wish to love. She did not wish to have a conversation on the sidewalk in front of a bar she had only visited twice, and once before with a former lover, and she did not wish for that conversation to lead to love. If she had known that conversation would lead to love she might have stayed home and put on her pajamas and watched movies on Netflix instead. It is not that Kate does not want to love. It is that when Kate loves, she does not walk the same in the world as when she does not love. When Kate does not love she can hold her shoulders back as if the horizon belongs to her. When Kate does not love, she can handle loneliness with showers and exercise and home-cooked food and nice lotion and good books and foreign movies. When Kate does love she does not know how to handle loneliness. When Kate loves, all former prescriptions for loneliness do not work.

Kate believes that most people believe that when there is love there is no longer loneliness. Kate thinks this is erroneous because Kate has never felt love without loneliness. Kate has found that love is loneliness the way love is also violence and life is blood.

I am going to tell you a story. This man, James, whom Kate loves, is an alcoholic who does not drink—there are many alcoholics who do not drink. They can be found in AA meetings, in offices, on subways, in homes, and driving cars. Many alcoholics who do not drink can be found in the list of past, current, and future lovers of people like Kate. Kate has considered that her love might make her lonely because she has loved men such as this man, James, but she has not considered that her love might make her lonely because she is human. She does not want to consider that to be human is to be lonely because that means there is no excusing her sadness, because then her sadness is a part of her. That means loneliness is a part of life. She wants to believe that her sadness, and her loneliness, could be blamed on James or on her past loves, because then it could, perhaps, end.

James is an alcoholic who does not drink. He chose not to drink before he met Kate and for reasons that have nothing to do with her. He met Kate on the sidewalk in front of a bar that he did not know she had been to twice before, and once with a former lover. James was in front of the bar because he works in front of the bar. He checks the IDs of alcoholics who drink and the IDs of people who are not alcoholics who want to drink beside alcoholics.

After James met Kate he asked for Kate's number and the next day he texted Kate. He said: I want to see you (he does not text things like I want to see you anymore). Now he does not text Kate at all. He texts other people instead. He taught her to expect him to text her and then he stopped texting her when she began to expect him to. But early on the day after the day when they spoke on the sidewalk in front of the bar, she was not expecting him to text her but he did. She replied to him that he should come over. He said he could not come over until late and then he did. They did not fuck. They did sleep in the same bed. Then they fucked in that same bed in the morning.

I am going to tell you a story. Kate has a wish about love because she did not wish to love. James loves Kate but he does not know what to do with love. James has things to do. James does not want to include Kate in his list of things to do. James's things to do include waking up, writing, listening to music, working out at the gym, going to an AA meeting or two, taking a walk, and going to work. James likes to do the things he likes to do alone. James does not like to be spoken to unless he is ready to be spoken to. James does not want to be contacted unless he reaches out first. James does not want Kate to initiate sex unless he initiates sex. James is a boundary.

James has a wish about love because he wishes to love and be loved but he does not know how to survive the loneliness in love. He wishes to love the way he knows that Kate loves him. He wishes that he could turn his mind outside of itself. He wishes he could learn how to live his life for someone else instead of thinking of what he has do next before work and whether he has nough money to buy the four dollar slice instead f the dollar slice and that he'll just text Kate later nd what train he will take into the city and vhether he looks scary to the woman who just rossed the street in front of him.

James does not text Kate anymore because ames knows that Kate expects him to. Kate exts Ed instead of James. Ed never expects Kate o text because Kate rarely texts Ed. Kate and Ed ave been friends for 12 years. Kate and Ed are n love. Kate loves loving Ed. Ed loves loving Kate. Ed lives in a different city than Kate. Kate nd Ed have kissed in the past, but Ed mostly refers kissing men. Kate feels more like herself vith Ed than she does with anyone, except naybe Mira. Mira is a character you don't know (Mira is a character you should know). Mira and Ed have never met, but they have heard stories bout each other from Kate. Mira met Kate before Kate met James and James has met Mira. ames resents that Mira resents James for not exting Kate. Kate resents that she cannot figure out if she wants James to text her or if she vants to be left alone (maybe she wants to be eft alone because she is already disappointed).

I am going to tell you a story. This story has a haracter named Mira. Mira is a teacher who alms children with stories and draws futures vith chalk. Kate loves Mira and Mira loves Kate (but they have never kissed). Mira gives Kate what Kate doesn't get from James. Ed gives Kate what ecrets are made to keep alive. Kate only knows now to be free with Ed and Mira. She wishes she ould be free with James, but it is hard to be free vith a boundary.

A plot: a young woman falls in love with an emotionally unavailable bouncer and seeks solace n friendships old and new.

When Kate has had enough of James being ames, she decides to spend more time with Mira.

Mira says she wants to love like Kate, full and hungry, and she tells Kate she might love Elisa. Kate believes in her, says she should let herself love, and at a party Elisa asks Kate if Mira is interested, really interested, and Kate says maybe? She thinks so? But Mira does not go home with Elisa, the way that Kate takes Mary home.

Elisa and Mary are new characters, also women. Elisa loves women and Mary loves men but she sometimes sleeps with women. Mira asks how it went with Mary, and Kate says it was fun but there's no future there. Mira wants to spend Valentine's together and so Kate says yes. They eat and hold hands and Mira says she is falling in love with someone else. Kate is hurt. Kate is devastated. Kate loves Mira more than Kate or Mira have understood.

[there is crying]

James still texts Kate sometimes. He wants the best for Kate even though he couldn't give Kate what she wanted. Kate, again, walks with her shoulders back as if the horizon belongs to her. Ed visits Kate and Kate misses Ed when he is away. Ed and Kate do not live together because Ed and Kate have chosen different cities, different people.

This story has an end: here, hi, this is the end (an end is really the beginning of mystery, the exit from what you can know to what you cannot). A story can tell you more, tell you less, tell you not much at all about what happens after the action. After the characters have shuffled out and away from each other. An end can point at a future, or close what came before. If it's good, maybe, it can do both. Mira and Kate do not speak anymore. James has new love and new love and new love because love that isn't new asks too much. Ed has solid love, good love, with someone where he lives. Kate has good love, solid love, with someone else too. So does Mira, so it seems to Kate, so she hopes for Mira, so she wishes for them all.

Jesse Salvo

Safe Seat

The news reports like grapeshot somewhere out in the darkness of the Richmond suburbs, it is the sort of story that railroads your day, that you must pay attention to even if you'd rather not: that the Senator has run somebody over with his car. The initial reports are so splashy, the ledework so cagily gleeful, soon everything must be caveated and hedged and walked-back in that nauseating rigamarolish way of the television news. Killed? In Critical Condition? In Traction? The initial testimonials definitely had said words like *Dead, Flattened, Crushed, Deceased, Mortal Coil*, etc. but now everyone's getting boots on the ground and no one (no legacy media, anyway) wants to be first through the wall. What is certain is that there was a human person that the Senator rolled over while piloting a vehicle. A car? Actually, no, as it turns out. The Senator is an accomplished dressageist, an equestrian fanatic (in terms of twists on already lurid news stories, this is like throwing a lit match on gasoline) it was a literal *coach-in-four* that he was driving (*why was he driving it himself?*) around some weird palatial estate in the Richmond Suburbs at 11pm on a Saturday when he rolled-over some unknown person or persons who now is/are in critical condition, or traction, or a body bag, somewhere in the greater D.C. area. Someone gets the erstwhile head of the American Equestrian Association hooked up to a lavalier. He says, "Horses are gentle animals of noble spirit that would never wilfully trample a person, despite all the propaganda." Apparently in the equestrian community there is a lot of concern over the negative portrayal of horses in media as heedless tramplers or ignoble beasts.

Your landlord who has been waiting for you after work the past couple of weeks has pasted a notice to your door. It is not an eviction notice you explain to your daughter with your brain somewhere south of your throat. It is a notice that you must show up to Housing Court, where people rarely ever actually get evicted. You don't know if this latter part is true or not but you recall a coworker saying it once on cigarette break.

It was 11pm on a Saturday during a recess period that the incident was reported, beggaring: was the Senator drinking? Was he drunk? Is it illegal to be piloting a horse (four horses) drunk? Someone goes and looks up an eighteenth-century statute regarding coachmen and valets but is unsure of whether it applies, jurisdictionally. How much responsibility might the horses have in all this? The head of the AEA says "none, full stop." but slip-and-fall lawyers online are openly speculating about whether the Senator could be said to have "lost control of the animals" and what it all might mean from a criminal or civil liability perspective.

Then there is the fact that he is in a safe seat. He should step down, surely, if it turns out his coach and four snuffed out some innocent pedestrian. The news, maddeningly, still will not confirm anything. The Senator's office issues a non-statement. The veteran legislator was involved in an "unfortunate occurrence" something something fully cooperating with police something something eager to get back to legislative session. The phrase "unfortunate occurrence" has a brief half-life as a joke passed between journalists and comedians and whoever else, then collapses in on itself, under the strain of the stories' sheer velocity.

The head of a splinter animal rights organization that PETA recently disavowed goes on live television and threatens to end his life if a single horse is euthanized. The host of the cable show he is appearing on makes a face at the camera like Can You Believe This? even though surely the host must have had prior approval of the guest panel of his own show, no? Someone dashes off a very quick editorial about how, were the Senator a person of color who had trampled somebody to death with his four dressage horses, e police would not be nearly as deliberative about elivering their personal version of justice. Everyody scratches their head and tries to be a good ally nd perform the democratic exercise of picturing uch a circumstance.

Whatever paste your landlord used to attach the otice has peeled off the door's front paint, so now ere are exposed patches of pre-war white on the oor's streaky red, which you are worried will be ken out of your deposit or used against you some-ow in Housing Court. Do you have to get a lawyer for ousing Court, or can you just represent yourself? ou don't want to show up to some full-fledged Evic-on proceeding looking your dowdiest and pretend-g to be Daniel Webster with some intimidating gov-rnment prosecutor on the other side, but you also emember the time you got fined by the cops for fall-g asleep on the train home and missing your stop nd ending up in the train depot. *That* proceeding ok place in a cramped little cubicle with a Jay Street ureaucrat and no cop or prosecutor on the other de, and you cannot afford to pay for a lawyer any-ay so this is all pretty academic, but *also* the one ing you can afford even less than a lawyer is being victed in the middle of the school year, right before ur daughter's school play (she is playing Daniel Vebster in *The Devil and Daniel Webster*—*Daniel*le Web-er—who you just found out about and now are re-lly learning to admire, as a historical person).

The estate where the accident occurred be-onged to the head of an investment group that lentifies and invests in "Emerging technologies" icluding, in 2009, a natural gas extraction tech-ique that poisoned a whole town somewhere ear the Smoky Mountains. The woman beside ne Senator in the coach-and-four was some phar-naceutical heiress who refuses to speak to the ress. The Senator's office releases a second, less nodyne, statement that reads "[He] will continue ighting for [his] constituents, [he] will not bow to ne vagaries of an online mob." You are looking up ne word vagaries on your phone even though you

are pretty sure you know what it means, when a man taps you on the shoulder and shows you a picture on his phone of himself naked and leering, and you begin shouting in order to attract attention and the man begins sprinting away from you down the bus station corridor and is tackled by a hotdog vendor.

It emerges that the Richmond Police breatha-lyzed the Senator upon arriving at the scene, where he sat slumped, dejected, reigns in hand, in the narrow trench of the coach-in-four's iron foot-board. You text your manager about trading shifts to get off to go to "an appointment." You do not want to say "to go to Housing Court" because A) it is embarrassing and B) your manager's perception of the stability of your home life might end up be-ing some ambient factor in considering whether you get more or less work, worse or better shifts, in the coming year, and whether or not you are con-sidered for a promotion or more responsibility, at some point down the line. "OK but U owe me 1" he says with a winky face which you do not like at all, either the rakish winky face or the implication of being owed or owing.

Whatever the results of the breathalyzer were, they have been thrown out. The police inexplica-bly just threw them out and no one is sure what to make of that. A Richmond PD spokesperson says they cannot release the name of any victim or vic-tims, it's a legal thing. But someone tracks down an old man in a hospital bed in Bethesda who says he was trampled by four horses being driven by someone who matches the Senator's description. The old man, who was an Uber driver summoned to the estate to pick up some charge, was wander-ing around the grounds staring at the GPS on his phone when suddenly he found himself sucked under the thundering hooves of four enormous creatures while above him two voices cackled. His pelvis is broken and also a shin bone. The old man says he forgives the Senator. He says, "Love is our only way out of this thing." He doesn't specify what this thing is, and nobody asks. Nor does anyone mention that the Senator hasn't actually asked for forgiveness.

You come upon a dim old woman crying in the hall by her doorway and you instruct your daughter, in her overlarge powdered wig and blue cutaway tailcoat, to carry the groceries inside and wait for you there. The old woman is clutching the same notice as was stuck to your door. You explain to her as you already did your daughter, that the notice does not mean she's being evicted but that she must show up to Housing Court. She asks where is Housing Court and you show her on your phone. She stares at it like it is the first phone she has ever seen. She asks how to get there, and if you have a car and can drive her. You tell her apologetically that you don't have a car. You somehow know—the same way you know when people say Pre-War, exactly which War they are referring to—that this old woman will lose her apartment.

The Senator is in a safe seat and could easily step aside and let the governor fill it in the interim. Some members of the state party have issued mealy-mouthed condemnations, but the august representative gets out there and presses the flesh, and announces instead he will "knuckle down and weather this storm." He announces "I will never stop fighting for you," which is you, you guess, as one of his constituents. His opponent in the next state election, you look up, is a former Tech CEO who believes in Thetan Levels and has advocated the wholesale dismantling of the FDA. Someone writes a long magazine piece about how the Senator's tender feelings about horses are linked to some wayback childhood trauma you didn't realize he'd suffered, and how he is trying "after one of the darkest, most humbling stages of his career, to rebuild his brand" and you guess how we are all human after all and deserving of love.

You are headed into Housing Court with your folder of various documents detailing rent moratoriums and prior payments and unfixed leaks

and some child on their phone spills her coffee o your voile blouse which you had paid to get dry cleaned. You arrive at the building and wander d rectionless around the halls like a doofus wit your stained shirt. It is hot and you are sweatin into your armpits and you ask a nearby man in security blazer where anything is. You find you courtroom, check the roster, and see that you hearing date has been moved to a month fror now. You are very hot and very annoyed and yo walk out onto the street but don't cry because th last time you cried was something special.

The legislative session is kicking up again an the ranking Senators are all talking about ho spending has been going crazy lately, and ho they will need to start bearing down, and reinin in the debt, and that will mean some hard choice for Americans. Your Senator, meanwhile, broker some deal to secure hundreds of PCB circuits fo small business startups all across the state. Yo don't know what PCB circuits are, but the report ing seems breathless, and everyone seems reall impressed with the Senator, and you guess tha small businesses could use some help probably.

You go see your daughter, in peruke and whit cummerbund, arguing some democratic cas against the Miltonian Satan. She remembers all o her lines and you are really proud and even almos cry a little. You take her out for steak which is he favorite food even though she is so small and it i weird to like steak. She has a small hand that fits i your hand softly and you love her so so much an you are scared of what happens if you die and she is alone in the world with hands that small. You are so scared of everything all the time and alway going wherever people tell you to, but you can tel she will not be that way. She will be brave and re member all her lines and will not have so muc trouble crying as you have. You come home to fin they've changed the locks on the door.

Matthew Tomkinson

Livn Inthwrld

My name is Livn Inthwrld. That's how it is. Please pay attention to me. I know the alphabet with 95% accuracy. The rest of you would all do well to forget it.

I'm also quite knowledgeable about the game of shogi. I've been learning from my older cousin for a while now, and I'm good at it. If you want to know more about the rules of the game, you'll have to look them up on your own time.

Here's something else: I like the sport of archery. I'm not good at much, but I'm good at hitting birds in the face. I have a few friends who share my love for the sport. Once a year, we get together and chat about it (plus some other things). We test out our skills in a game of popinjay. But don't think that the birds aren't on my side. If I had a parrot, it would be sitting on my head right now as I write this.

If you want to know something, just ask me.

I was born in the county of Aue, which lies next to Luson. In summer, we have all kinds of festivals in our hometown. In winter, I look at the sky through my special glasses. If there's a thunderstorm, I try to see it. I get very annoyed when there are no stars or planets.

I recently found out about a constellation made up of Three Sisters. They are named Alnitak, Alnilam, and Mintaka. I think those are perfect names. With my telescope I can count all 96 bags of urine left behind by astronauts on the moon. They're easy enough to spot from my backyard.

I love going to the countryside and taking walks on the frozen river at night. The sound of the ice cracking under my feet is almost as pleasant as the cracking of my voice. There are usually a few pairs of people there, near the river, two or three couples on bicycles and often one tall man walking alone, the kind who walks away from a group to do his business in the woods. I always wonder why he walks so far from the others.

One time my mother and I were out hiking, and she saw an open square of light somewhere in the trees ahead of us. It was an opening onto another world. And if I turned my head a certain way, I could picture a skull lying among the bushes.

"And if I turned my head a certain way, I could picture a skull lying among the bushes."

Isn't that a pretty cool line?

I don't mean to brag, but my mother is an artist, though she has not made any new art in a long time. Then there's my father, who's in charge of fashion. He used to make perfume for my mother using rose petals from a garden where he once worked as a youth. They make a good couple. My mother loves the shape of certain vases, and my father has a certain vase-like shape about him.

No offense to my parents, but my favourite living relative is my sick sister Marfa (Marfuh). She sleeps with her eyes open. She likes to read books with her pupils fully dilated, especially the ones about volcanoes. I always wake her up with a little song.

She believes that my soul is that of a medieval pauper. I sometimes get the impression that she's right.

You know, I almost never go shopping. When my family asks me if I want anything, I always say no, because if there's something that makes me happy, then buying that thing will inevitably make me sad, with books being no exception.

My father's brother used to own a literary magazine. He had quite the beard, and very strange glasses. He used to live with us, but now he lives alone in another building miles away from here. He has a birdcage full of finches. I can hear them singing when he puts out corn for them in the morning.

Here's a funny story about my uncle: he just got a new car, and bragged to his friends all about it at dinner. The next day, he took his family to the countryside for a drive and crashed into the railings on both sides of the bridge and hit another car passing by, headed in the opposite direction.

If I remember correctly, our first family vehicle was a Jeep. The brakes used to squeak horribly. When it rained and the windshield wipers were on, you couldn't tell which sounds came from the wipers and which came from the brakes.

I almost forgot to tell you that no one was seriously injured. In the crash, I mean.

Come to speak of it, another little bit of blood has appeared in my bedroom, which means there must be something nearby with a big cut on its body. Lately, an ant has been crawling around the baseboards, looking for a place to die, some way for its life to end. But the blood can't possibly belong to him. There's too much of it.

Perhaps a little bear wandered in here. We like to keep all the doors open in the spring, so it's not impossible.

A bear is one of the nicest creatures to look at, wouldn't you say? They don't do anything bad to people, and they're so deliciously round. I've never understood why people are so afraid of them. But then again...

Once a year, I used to go on an excursion with my grandfather to visit old caves. I admired the way the stalactites and stalagmites grow towards each other. The caves alway have narrow passages, so you have to go ve slowly, stooping a little.

I miss my grandfather. He was my family' greatest treasure. Before he passed away, I wen to see him for the first time in a long while. He was sitting on a mound of sand looking into the distance. "Sometimes I think it would be bette if everything we did was restricted to the sur face layer of the planet. But please don't make me think about this too hard," he said. Then he got up and walked off without looking back.

Once, years later, my father took me to visi his grave at the foot of the mountains. But after hours of searching, we still couldn't find it. Yesterday I was out that way with my friends, looking at the larkspurs. They were in full bloom, and their petals reminded us of something underwater.

How many times must I say it? I'm not afraid of dying in the mountains. My greatest fear is dying on a table. I've seen my relatives strapped to tables before. The needles are thick like caterpillars. The cold mountain air feels like a million of them undulating on my skin.

Dear reader, I'm sorry to cut things short but I have to go get ready for tonight. It's my birthday dinner, and afterwards we're going to spend the evening at Sarcophagus Park. I want you to know that I will be saying my prayers for you before the meal.

For what it's worth, I'm sorry that I write in such a strange way. Sometimes my mind is full of tears. The kind of tears that rhyme with bears. I just like to be alone sometimes and put my thoughts down on paper every once in a while, when my family's not looking. That way they don't get lost inside my head. My family, I mean.

Ben Pester

square / recess / moon

Can you see those towers down there, on the other side of the city? That's where he was living at the time. In one of those angled-together buildings. I can't tell you which one, but he was definitely high up in the towers there. I know because he told me about it a lot. Also, I live around there too. Different tower, but I know the general area.

Ah now—yes. I see you have an address. I'm guessing you have tried to go there. I'm so sorry about this—really I am. OK, well it's worth a look I guess. Let me see? Yeah, that's what I thought—you have a street number, but that's just the building. I'm sorry. You don't know which apartment? It's not possible then. They cross over inside, those places. The textile workers or whoever they were who built that place hundreds of years ago, they built it like a circuit-board in there. All the apartments had these connections to other apartments, families with direct pathways to one another. Lanes of childcare access through the hearts of several buildings. Connections that mean nothing to us now. If I were you, I'd leave it well alone. If it helps put your mind at rest, I will describe the place.

In every apartment, I can tell you, there is a sort of living space that nobody uses. You don't use it, there's no light. You dump your stuff there if you have any stuff, and that's it. Sometimes, if you've lost your keys or a jacket, it might be in that dark room, but generally you stay out of it. There's a sort of feeling in that room that is not nice. A historical feeling, one with its connection broken. Does that make sense? Not much of it will. There is a bed-

room, which is a place for being unconscious in and nothing else. And then in every apartment, without exception, there is a good, warming kitchen. He liked the kitchen.

'Sometimes,' he said to me once, 'I find it hard to get out of the kitchen. Or, not the kitchen, but the dining area of the kitchen.'

This was about a month before he stopped turning up at work.

We were out for lunch when he told me about the dining area in his kitchen. It was my idea to go out for lunch in a bar—he wasn't the type to instigate it—though he said yes quickly enough. There was something automatic about the way he agreed to things, you know? As though agreeing to come for lunch was something he desperately craved, and yet could not articulate or arrange for himself. Some people are like that—but they get by. He came here alone, that tells me something—at some point this was someone who *decided* to come here. He had enough propulsion to pack a bag, and to set off. He had it in him to choose.

Sorry. Sorry for that pause—I think about him a lot, but it's hard to imagine him choosing things, taking control. I try to picture his face as he makes a decision but, I can't. I'm sorry. This is not why you came.

Anyway, I wanted a long lunch. I needed to get out of the office, if you want the truth. The place was dying around us. I was badly in need of a distraction from the work I was failing to do. Our friend always seemed to be up to date with his projects. He could always make time for extra meetings and so on so I dragged him out with me. He was unaffected by the obvious calamity of our company's situation. He turned up, smiled at the right time, did his work, let it all wash over him. He was a lifeboat in a sea of dead boats—that's how I saw him then any way. Does that make sense?

I'll continue. We were day drinking, as I have said. The company we worked for was not progressing well. We were circling the drain, and even though there was financing, there was nothing going on in the sales team. It was a depressing situation, but it didn't affect him. Not at all. I think he planned to just work there, do his level best, until the place went under. Then I imagine he would have expected to find somewhere else he could quietly sit and carefully, efficiently, re-evaluate the technology stack of a new company that was wasting money and couldn't understand why. There is a lot of work in this town. A lot of work and not much else. Well, towers, obviously. Plenty of towers.

Anyway, that lunchtime we went to the bar across the square from the office. I didn't tell him this, but I planned to drink the whole afternoon. I needed company.

The place was called *Gerrards*. It was one of those bars that crop up within the ground floor of large office buildings. You enter through a heavy smoked glass door into an open space, walled with more smoked glass. The bar staff are interchangeable with the reception staff in the business entrance on the other side of the building. The toilets for the bar are actually the guest toilets for the meeting rooms on the first floor and basement.

We sat on a sofa eating chips. I tried to move things along, but he just wanted bottles of beer, slow drinking, to his credit—he didn't mind that I was doubling his pace. He didn't mind.

He was silent. No choice really, trying to look interested while I held forth about how I was going to get sacked or the company was going to go under and I didn't know which was coming first. After a while I became sick of hearing myself talk, so I asked him about himself, how he was finding things. I was on the verge of begging him to talk to me about anything, anything at all, just to keep me from whining. And that was how he started talking about that room of his. The dining area of the kitchen.

'I can't stop thinking about it,' he said. 'I thin[k] about being in that room all the time. Like, I neve[r] really leave. Or I do, but somehow I don't.'

I found this a very odd thing to say, of cours[e] but I told him, 'That's normal. That's totally nor mal. You're in a new town. You need something t[o] anchor you. It's totally normal to like a room.'

'Yes. I suppose that's true,' he said, but he didn[t] seem satisfied. Then he said, 'I keep a little ver[-] bena plant on a shelf, just below the window There's a table with two chairs, one of which [I] think of as the main chair, it faces straight out [of] the window, across the table. That's my chair.'

'So, if I ever come over, I'll sit on the other chai[r] then will I?'

He didn't really hear me. He went on describin[g] the room. He moved his hands to where the vari ous features of this room were in proportion t[o] where we were sitting. He closed his eyes on cer tain words, nodding as if to confirm to himself, ye[s] this is *window*. Yes, here is *chair*. I found myself re laxing into the idea of this room.

'The curtains are a kind of rust red,' he told me 'Linen they are, thin enough to blow in the breeze and to let the moon glow through—where th[e] weave is thicker, the material fractures the ligh[t] ever so gently. The walls are the colour of butter, o[r] yellowed ivory, and made of this bulky, soft mor tar.' He stroked his cheek as he talked about th[e] walls, and I realised he was imagining it agains[t] his skin. 'I can't describe what it's made of, the wal[l] plastering, I don't have the words, but it is like art It's like a sculpture in plaster, everything is smooth and organic like a softened cave.'

At this point I was just nodding along. It's od[d] isn't it? But I was no longer embarrassed. I shoul[d] have been because who talks like this? But yo[u] have to understand, I could see that room—there i[s] the window, the sky beyond it, the tiles on the roof[s] outside like the rippling tides of a sea. There is th[e] old plaster, butter yellow. I can close my eyes and see it all now, just as I describe it to you.

'It's so nice,' I told him. Even through the booze, I was deadly serious, this room now sounded like heaven to me.

'The walls have these recesses which form incidental shelves. I have a lamp in one of these. In the evenings, I put the lamp on and it glows in the little recess—it looks like a sentry there, chubby in the recess. The night air comes in and mixes the fragrance of the city with the soft citrus of the verbena plant.'

I had my eyes closed by now. I felt myself there completely as he told me about the floor tiles, how cool they were. He told me again, but in a new way about how the light hit the roofs that lay below the window and all around. The tiles like a sea.

We came to a natural break in the description of the room, and then it was just us again, sitting together in this weird numbness. I slapped my legs, got him another beer.

After that, we spoke regularly, but we didn't go out together again. Whenever we found ourselves alone together, I made sure the emphasis of the chat was firmly back on the shit state of things in the company—which is to say, I did all the talking. He would drop something in from time to time. He got into the habit of telling me about the book he was reading, which in fact he had been struggling with since he'd found it in his apartment when he moved here.

It was about a couple of fictional mountaineers, his book. They were climbing a deadly, unscalable mountain. I think the idea was that somehow this mountain was bigger than Everest, and it had come in the night, or something. A sudden, weird mountain. Very far-fetched, very pointless. Anyway, this vast thing that dwarfed the mighty Everest was being climbed by two mountaineers, but get this—the whole book wasn't even about how this fictional mountain came to be there. It was instead about the toxic relationship between these two climbers. This intensely damaged relationship the climbers had with each other was the focus of the whole story. At one point—I think this is right—several hundred bats the size of men emerged from a cave and beset them, tearing at their flesh, but the scene was forgotten after barely half a page, the bats having been easy to kill with crampons and ice hacks. After that, he told me, for a hundred more pages they were just teasing each other, and claiming petty victories of spite—insulting each other's table manners, being offensive about the smell they had, or one of them claiming to have swindled money from the other's parents. Always bringing each other down emotionally, working tirelessly to harm the confidence of the other mountaineer, so progress was painfully slow. For the sake of winning these increasingly petty quarrels, they risked losing limbs, even death. A load of shit.

He told me it was agony to read it, but he was determined to get to the end. 'Like being a mountaineer yourself,' I joked.

'Yes!' He agreed. 'Exactly, I think that might be the point of the book.'

Anyway, I was fine hearing about it, but then he told me how he read it mostly at home, in a large recess in the wall of the dining area of his kitchen. As soon as he told me about sitting there, with this dreary book, I could see it, the little recess just big enough for him to fit in there, the smooth plaster on the walls, the leaves of the verbena rustling softly. I could see the light, soft as cream, blending from the moon to the little lamp in its own recess, to the gentle burn of the gas hob. I felt as though I was there with him. I felt that embarrassment again, followed by a wave of sudden weariness.

I had to slap myself in the legs again to snap out of it. Then he let me rage on about the state of the company, the woolliness of the CEO, how I had lost all confidence in the place, how things were falling apart around us and we didn't have any way of stopping it—I was boring myself to be honest. We parted ways at the end of that particular day and from then on I stayed away from him—not wanting to bring him down, that's what I told myself, but also I began to find it harder and harder to be around him. Whenever he spoke, he would mention his room. And I felt hypnotised, found myself enveloped there with him, embarrassed and fatigued.

I few weeks later, I found him in a state of quite serious distress—he was late to the office, something that almost never happened. I assumed he was just sick or feeling tired. I had been feeling bad for neglecting him. Taking some of those assholes from the QA team out for drinks instead of inviting him. He hadn't said anything, but he kept meeting my eye, and I would smile and find excuses to be somewhere else. Awful of me, I'm sorry.

I found him in the breakout room. He was sitting at the white table staring straight ahead into space. He looked a wreck, I'm sorry to say. His hair was out of shape. He had a smell coming off him. I didn't realise he'd noticed I was even there until he began speaking.

'I felt myself fading away,' he said. 'I don't know what's happening to me.'

'What do you mean fading away? Like passing out?'

'No. Not passing out. I was in a queue and, after a while I realised I had been waiting so long, I couldn't remember what the queue was for. I was just standing there behind this tall man, somehow I couldn't manoeuvre myself out of the line to see what was at the other end. The tall man kept moving too. Nobody would move out of my way.'

'Jeez, we've all been there,' I said. 'I *fade out*, as you call it, all the time in queues. You're probably just tired. Head home maybe?'

'No it wasn't like that. I literally didn't know the time of day. It could have been a lunch place or a coffee truck. The queue went round the corner of the building—I had no idea what was going on. And I then I could smell verbena. I could hear the curtains flapping in the breeze.'

'Eh?'

'I could feel the tiles beneath me, I could feel the sun gradually moving across the table. I could see the little lamp like a man in the recess. I saw the sun move, and the leaves of the verbena grew. I was there for hours. I cleaned the table, I touched the walls . . .'

'I think we need to get outside somewhere,' I told him.

I took him under the arm and hurried him out of the break-out room towards the exit, and into a lift.

I couldn't explain to him at the time, but as he was speaking, I myself had lost focus. I had found myself in his room—the dining area of his kitchen—or not actually in the room, but I felt the sense of the room. My friend's sad eyes had turned away from me as he spoke, and for an instant, I couldn't see him at all. The room was there instead.

Outside in the square, the city noise and the cool air cleared my head slightly.

'Are you alright?' I asked. 'You feeling better out here?'

'Better,' he said.

He did not look better at all. He looked panicked. I wanted to leave him there. His window and the verbena plant flickered as he stood there. I wanted to run away and never speak to him again, but I could not. It wasn't his fault, whatever was going on.

I put my arm through his, and we walked through the square and off towards the South City Road. After some time, as we dodged around the mid-morning crowd, he spoke again.

'You're the only person I speak to in this town. I don't speak to a single other living soul.' We were essentially lost in the streets when he said this. I was trying to get a grip, but I dared not look at him in case he was a curtain.

'That's no good!' I said. 'No friends? We'll have to fix that! You always look so happy in the office. Or at least, contented. I assumed you had people!' I was lying, it was clear that he had no people. I felt dreadful.

'You gave me a bit of a scare,' I said after he seemed to have calmed down.

'I'm better now,' he said.

'Are you sure?'

'Yes, I want to go home.'

I walked him home and we didn't say anything else. I didn't look at him, not even to say goodbye as he slipped through his doorway in the white base of the towers.

The next day he was mugged outside on the street. I don't know exactly what happened—he told me about it, but he couldn't give me the full details. Someone rushed him from behind, shoved him to the ground, took his bag, took his wallet. Left his phone. He didn't say anything else about it—not the exact location, no description of the mugger, nothing.

I know that he had several important documents taken from him. Precious objects, he called them. Documents and pictures.

'They didn't see me at all,' he said. He was talking about being at the police station, where they don't stand on politeness the way I might. He tried to report the crime, but they didn't see him. They saw a window. Do you understand? He was talking but they saw roof tiles, they saw a pleasant sky.

He was saying pictures of my daughter. He was saying my life has been stolen, but they saw plaster and they smelled verbena.

Eventually he had to leave the police station. He tried making a phone call but leaves closed instead. The curtains blew in the wind.

I spoke to him that night. He contacted me through the work messaging system, which I stupidly have on my phone. I agreed to meet up.

He said he wanted to have dinner so we went to a Chinese place near the towers. Good food. Cheap.

He was alright eating. We talked about dumb stuff. Some work gossip. He said he felt bad for Ollie, a young guy who had recently joined. He worked late every day, but nobody would promote him because there was no money.

'Why doesn't he get it?' he said. 'Silly idiot!'

It was the first serious work conversation I had ever had with him.

'Don't you want to talk about the police?' I asked. 'You were mugged. What happened?'

But he didn't want to talk about it. Instead, we talked about the book shop in town, what they had in the window there. We talked about the fountains in the park.

For a while the cold moon shone through and cast the wooden table in a broad paleness. The verbena shivered in the cold. I had to go to the bathroom and wash my face.

It seemed that when he was eating he held up OK.

'I still don't know anything about you really,' I said to him. 'What do you like doing?'

He started talking, but instead of him, there was the window. There was the table and the best chair facing the window. There was the lamp. Over to my right was the hob. He was saying something but there were clouds processing over the distant chimneys, the creak of a beetle investigating the soil of the plant pot. I watched for a long time as the moon in the dining area of his kitchen completely replaced his face.

When he finally spoke again, he said, 'I like swimming. I love to swim but I haven't seen anywhere in this town that suits me.'

Determined not to see the room again, I asked him if he'd tried the sorrel centre.

'I've tried. But, too many people. Too much of a crowd'

'What about over in South Point?'

'I tried to get there, but the place was closed. It looked good though. Quiet.'

We agreed to go down to south point for a swim soon. I felt weird agreeing to this. He sensed my hesitation, I think, because he said, 'Look I'll be there at Six AM tomorrow. If you can't make it, don't worry. But I'll be there. I need to at least have the appointment—it will motivate me,' he said.

'Really? Six AM tomorrow?'

'Six AM! Oh yeah!'

He tried to make it sound like a joke, but I could hear a snag in his voice, like he was actually quite nervous about what would happen to him in a swimming pool. Would someone drown as they swam out towards the blue sky above the rooftops?

'Six AM!' I said. 'I'll be there.'

'It'll be great!' He was actually smiling.

'I can't promise to match your sunny mood!'

'Haha!'

'Haha!'

We stayed for drinks at the Chinese place, which was a mistake because I lost concentration and for a long time the curtains billowed, the red rust curtains, the verbena plant on the shelf under the window hushed as cool air and the night fragrance of the city came in, clouds pushed shadows across the butter yellow walls, the lamp squatted like a little man in the silver light, guarding his recess in the wall. I felt the sudden sensation that I was falling, plummeting into ice, because in the

room was a figure, a hand wiping dust from the table—a terrible horrible sadness came over me.

'Six AM!' my friend said again. The sadness lifted instantly. His face, his cheery face saying stupid time of the morning, was back.

I never made it to the swimming pool. I haven't seen him since that night in the Chinese restaurant, but I'm telling you, he's in that room. That what I'm saying, it makes no difference, I have no idea where exactly his room is. It's a maze in there you could try all week and never find it. Even if you have the address, the address is no good, I told you that. The whole place crosses over and repeats, like a ritual. And in every apartment, in every space, a room so tranquil, so utterly harmonious that if you're not careful it will replace you.

But you already know that because right now I see the sun going down through a window, a chair turning grey in silhouette. I am talking to you but the curtain is flapping in the breeze, the plaster is butter yellow.

You are listening but there is now just a window. You are listening but there is only a table set in front of the window, a bat flickers past changing direction, rippling the air. The roof tiles shrink in the cold.

A window a table a recess with a lamp.

A window a table.

A moon looking in.

The figure is there. The figure, starved and tall grumbles by the table, shuffling, wrapped tightly in material. The figure moves slowly, casting hideous shadows, devouring the light into its mouth, dusting the table, cooking beans. The figure there all day, running long obsessive hands over the verbena plant—hours go by, days go by the figure, the window the ocean of the tiles on the roofs that scale the lost and most forlorn night.

Polymorphous Polyester

Sterling Karat Gold
Isabel Waidner
Peninsula Press (UK), June 2021

As with Waidner's previous novels *Gaudy Bauble* and *We Are Made Of Diamond Stuff*, the setting of Sterling Karat Gold is modern Britain, and we are given physical co-ordinates of where to find the streets and tower blocks where the action is occurring. This grid is no more based in conventional realism than the picture-boxes of a graphic novel provide the structure of linear narrative. The universe of these books is like that of the graphic novel, with fantastic transformations occurring at the edges of sharply-rendered, embodied emotions and reaction moments. The register slides quickly and without warning from comic to absurd to factual and meditative.

There could be room for illustrations in these books, as there were in Ann Quin's final novel *Tripticks*, or in some of Jeff Nuttall's works. That earlier tradition of "experimental" fiction was acknowledged briefly in *Diamond Stuff*, but it has little direct influence here, neither in the style nor in the identities of the narrators. When these characters get to speak, they are "clear" and "forthright" as any "normal" person; they simply do not often get the opportunity to connect outside the worlds they are held in. The one direct "literary" source is from parts of Kafka's *Trial*, acknowledged in the text. Kafka's characters, when located in modern buildings, are usually the well-to-do, surprised to find themselves brought down and demoralised by the bureaucratic underworld they usually existed above and apart from. These characters have been caught in its meshes their entire lives, lives punctuated by documents and interviews and interrogations, identities always on trial.

The theme running through these stories is "representation", in all its senses. The sense of political representation and being spoken for or advocated by lawyers or activists; the sense of portrayal in art and popular culture, through stereotypes and conventional motifs whose significance can be lost in time; the formal representations in Google streetmaps, linking frozen, obfuscated moments with the formal cartography of Ordnance Survey; the use and reuse of artefacts and replicas as imitations. Images can become rebellious and activated without an observer, and act outside of their creators' intentions. Elaborate images can also stand in symbolically for cruder realities, reversing the usual direction of satire. Twice in this book, street confrontations are presented as bullfights. The staged, ritualised slaughter of a beast undangerous until driven by provocation, is bringing out the meaning of harassment as a ritual against lone members of minorities. Bullfights are not "literally" occurring in the streets of Camden. The reality of those scenes is their emotional atmosphere, rendered through the diagram of the violence. The repetition is the repetition of the cycle of abuse and aggression. A judge is "a tall, blue-bodied frog, spindly, with the head of a fledgling bird"—possibly a play on the old Cockney slang "up before the Beak".

In the loop of re-enactments, style can be a mark of resistance and signal of identity, which can also mystify even its familiars:

> Having dropped Chachki off at their block, I continue walking up Delancey towards mine, and the exact same person, Chachki, or so it seems, who I dropped off seconds ago, is now walking towards me, talking and gesticulating with urgency. Not only is this Chachki, so-called, positioned impossibly in relation to where I just left

them, they are dressed in an outfit entirely unfamiliar to me, namely a too-tight, cheap-looking, two-tone polyester two-piece, second-hand-car-dealer-style, and tassel loafers, which arguably counts as a look, somewhere, New Jersey. They've got their hair sleeked into a centre-parting, and, unfairly, are showcasing a neatly clipped pencil moustache, the likes of which I've been trying to grow for a decade but haven't been able to, and, more to the point, doesn't exist above Chachki's upper lip either, or it didn't seconds ago, and, what's the smell, is that eau de cologne?

There is a happy ending, or at least a denouement, and dissenting voices can be heard in its audience. The characters act as themselves.

REVIEW | Jesi Buell

Strange Bloodlines

Begat Who Begat Who Begat
Marcus Pactor
Astrophil Press, November 2021

*B*egat Who Begat Who Begat is a collection of short stories about parenthood with a perspective on the fractal nature of overlapping genetic roles: of being both parent and child. Pactor explores lineage and familial ties by weaving otherworldly and dreamlike elements into the mundane everyday. His skill with the surreal distinguishes this work from many other books about family relationships. A Freudian could have a field day with this collection, but so could anyone interested in work that challenges readers through experimentation in form, imagery, and language.

While other family members feature as characters in these stories, the two most important relationships are where the narrator interacts with a father or with a daughter. For these narrators, the father tends to function as a reflection while the daughter repre-

sents the radically Other; both are contiguous and yet somehow still foreign. In the stories "Harvest" and "Do the Fish," the narrator understands the daughter by juxtaposing her with robots and AI. This comparison is not so much a 'real world vs. made world' dichotomy the narrative tries to espouse, as it is a construct the father uses to distance himself from his daughter's sexuality. The narrator often wants to 'save' the daughter from herself and her desires, but these impulses tell us more about the father's insecurities than it does about her.

The memories (real or imagined) of a father figure function similarly. In many stories, the father is a flawed individual, failing professionally or running over the dog with the family car or leaving a child behind. Despite these shortcomings, the narrator in each story still holds a deep love and respect for the father figure. His anger, sadness, and devotion towards this parent live all together in him. At different points, the narrator's memories of his father are mixed, but overall they carry a heavy sadness. Several times, the narrator acknowledges how imprecise and distorted his recollections might be, implying that there was a greatness there that he has simply forgotten. In "Archaeology of Dad," the text literally reflects the father's descent from glory as well as the imperfect memories of his child with large black holes, voids that the narrator tries to fill in with his own story. Fathers and daughters come to matter less as individual characters and more as presences or absences that the narrator uses to understand and to complete his own life story.

Pactor's writing has a Charlie Kaufman sadness and worry as well as unconventional narratives of Can Xue. Particular gems in this collection include: "Harvest," "Archaeology of Dad," and "The Remainder". If you like Diane Williams or Jorge Luis Borges and if you don't mind reading something that will make you think about your own family dynamics, you'll enjoy this inventive and bittersweet collection.

Public Reading Followed by a Discussion
Danielle Mémoire (tr. K.E. Gormley)
Dalkey Archive, April 2021

One of the more mercurial figures in French letters, Danielle Mémoire has been publishing since the mid-eighties, and with this volume, we have the chance at last to read her in English translation, courtesy of the recently revivified Dalkey Archive Press, under new management following the passing of founder John O'Brien. The novel opens with a public reading that is not a public reading and a Q&A that is not a Q&A, narrated by unnamed narrators who may or may not be the author, and audience members who may or may not be audience members. "Mémoire's works are examples of ludic literature," Warren Motte writes in the introduction, an understatement of *proportions énormes*, as the novel fragments into excerpts from the narrator's work-in-progress, excerpts that themselves contain writers making public readings that are not public readings and asking Q&As that are not Q&As. The novel proceeds in the manner of Barth's story "Meneliad," where frame tales are framed within frame tales like a sequence of nested algorithms, yielding prose that is intentionally and hilariously unfollowable.

As translator K.E. Gormley notes in her introduction, there are "struggles for dominance on the level of language itself, most notably between its spoken and written forms", as the fragments reach for levels of enlightenment and erudition by deploying italicised quotes, while others present interrogatory dialogues that penetrate into the narrator's more trivial utterances. Mémoire's novel plays out as a literary text commenting on the notion of a literary text as a form of self-interrogation, placing her novel in the same wheelhouse as surfictionists *à la* Raymond Federman in *Take It or Leave It*, a text that made the telling of the telling of as much importance as the telling of the tale itself. The reader's own take on whether the telling of (or telling-off) the text is as important as a tip-top tale well-told is proportional to that reader's interest in Dalkey Archive Press. A cross between the playful madness of the vintage Oulipo and the more sombre introversion of the nouveau romanciers, *Public Reading Followed by a Discussion* is a sublimely maddening introduction to an extremely welcome voice in translation.

Bedraggling Grandma with Russian Snow
João Reis (tr. by the author)
Corona/Samizdat, June 2021

As in the cinematic weirdscapes of Quentin Dupieux, where murderous rubber tyres stalk the land and style-obsessed men fawn over deerskin coats, Portuguese author João Reis creates hermetically sealed worlds of singular weirdness that inhabit their own surreal illogic and invite the reader to either step inside or scurry for cover under saner fictions. In his second Englished novel (self-translated from the original *A Avó e a Neve Russa*), Reis opens with two detectives discussing the murder of a 29-year-old woman (reported as in her 30s in the paper) with a plush donkey (a robo-toy created by the father of Alexei, whom the toy refers to as 'Dad'). Opening with the retelling of a breakfast where Alexei's father is keen to assert his right to call pancakes waffles, the plush donkey continues to digressively relate his memories of the morning.

The narrative floats away from the plush donkey to an unnamed narrator, into the run-on thoughts of Detectives Anderson & Mercier. The second part of the novel is a sustained interrogation of suspect Didier H., a section that brings to mind Dupieux's *Au Poste!*, a film centred around an increasingly absurd interrogation. Here, Detective Anderson's fixation on the works of Wittgenstein and works on Wittgenstein leads him to conduct a hilarious interrogation based on an overly literal rendering of Wittgensteinian logic, all the while blissfully unaware his co-detective has long been bedding his missus.

Reis's last book in English, *The Translator's Bride* (Open Letter), centred around a translator who smelled sulphur, and showed the author's skill at the crazed internal monologue form as perfected by Thomas Bernhard—an uproarious work of sustained coddiwompling in short, hiccupping clauses ensnuggled in commas. This novel is more liberal in its formal merriment, moving often randomly into long unpunctuated streams of consciousness, sequences of barmy interrogatory dialogue, and the repetitive rhythms of the extremely loveable plush donkey. A merry manglement of the sleuth procedural, the identity of the murderer is not as important (Reis tortures the reader with the murder's reveal) as the rollicking ride to nowhere in which the novel revels. A splendidly unhinged slice of surrealist noir.

You are Beautiful and You are Alone:
The Biography of Nico
Jennifer Otter Bickerdike
Faber & Faber (UK), Hachette (US), July 2021

Prior, the only superlative book on Nico was James Young's *Songs They Don't Play on the Radio*, an acid-tongued memoir of touring with the singer in the 1980s that depicted her in hilariously unflattering terms as a narcissistic junkie. This robustly researched bio succeeds in providing a more sober overview of the complex, tortured cult icon. Nico, born Christa Päffgen in 1938, was placed in a Nazi-run boarding school in her toddling period, after which she suffered extreme hunger in bomb-scorched Berlin, her playground a hellscape of bodies under rubble and vague memories of a father who fought on the wrong side. As in the vivid dystopian novels of J.G. Bal-lard—whose youth was partially spent in a Shang-hai internment camp—this early experience of horror, decay, and rootlessness came to inform her lugubrious and challenging music several decades later.

Her strange voyage from über-blonde pin-up and peripheral star of *La Dolce Vita* to touring Eastern Europe with suicide music is stylishly explored in Bickerdike's empathetic bio. Relying on her striking appearance to support her mother, Nico is increasingly used and spurned by her lovers (Alain Delon still refuses to acknowledge the son, Ari, that he had with Nico in the early 1960s), and has a series of strangely passionless romps with the likes of Bob Dylan, Jackson Browne, and Lou Reed. The swinging sixties is not a place for Nico to find stability. The era of free love, no attachments, or social boundaries leads predictably to her companionship with heroin for the next twenty years. Her 1970s are spent largely in an apartment with blacked-out walls with French auteur Philippe Garrel (who casts Nico in several avant-garde films).

Following her combative turn with the Velvet Underground, Nico spontaneously purchases a harmonium, the instrument on which she would compose songs for her whole career. In close collaboration with John Cale (most of Nico's best work has Cale's brilliant arrangements), she produced the seminal records *The Marble Index*, *Desertshore*, and *The End*, which represent the apex of her achievement—hauntingly bleak albums that resurrect spectres from the Dark Ages with the power of Dead Can Dance or Cocteau Twins. Tormented by her own beauty, she revelled in riddling her body with needle marks and rotting her teeth with heroin, rebelling steadfastly against the looks she had exploited in her early life, meeting the inevitable roar of misogyny heaped upon her by the music press.

Bickerdike, assisted by a cache of fresh interviews with Paul Morrissey, Iggy Pop, and Nico's son Ari, vividly evokes the world of rock from the 1960s onwards, an infantile playground for damaged ouls who had their nihilistic self-destruction cheered as some form of artistic transgression. Any listener to *Desertshore* will hear a childlike vulnerability mingled with the terror of the post-war chaos whence she was whelped. Bickerdike's gracefully rendered portrait of an artist who on the surface may seem arch or unlikeable, shows Nico a lost child nomadically wandering an uncaring world searching for a home, nebulising her traumas into heroin and breathtaking music. In her later years, she found in Manchester the closest thing to a home—in one touching account, Nico befriends a local Manc who accepts her for the first time as a friend without any ulterior motives. The simplicity of this connection shows how venal and superficial the world Nico inhabited was, and how powerfully she fought to assert her identity as an artist. A scintillating work of candour, passion, and empathy, this is an essential read for the Nico-curious.

A Very Strange Man: A Memoir of Aidan Higgins
Alannah Hopkin
New Island Books (Ireland), April 2021

In 1987, novelist/journalist Alannah Hopkin and modernist titan Aidan Higgins settled into their home in the town of Kinsale on the southern coast of Ireland, having struck up their romance the winter before c/o the matchmaking skills of poet Derek Mahon. Their home at slight remove from the sea was to become their main residence for the rest of Higgins's stint in this realm. Here, he completed one story collection, a book of travel pieces, one novel, a three-volume memoir on his childhood and life's loves, and a short book on the perils of blindness. Hopkin, twenty-two years younger, chose to concentrate on journalism to help support them.

A lucid memoir of two writers with fierce personalities cohabiting, Hopkin presents an iridescent insight into the crankiness, kindliness, and candour of a writer whose fiction was a form of baroque autobiography, whether the loss of grandeur in *Langrishe, Go Down* (based on the Higgins clan's sliding social status), the epic European sprawl of wanderlust in *Balcony of Europe* (informed by Higgins's wide travels), or the epistolary exchange of love-missives in *Bornholm Night-Ferry* (drawn from his relationship with a Danish poet). Hopkin creates an intimate portrait of a writer prone to acidic outbursts (his comments on Hopkin's own writing are a mix of helpful and offensive—she would publish no fiction until after his death), uninterested in modern culture (no TV in the house, niche musical tastes), a cool raconteur prone to social gaffes, and a mild-mannered and loving man content in his cocoon of literary eccentricity, frequently furious at the marginalisation of his talents by a predictably unreceptive public.

Higgins's medical decline is a catalogue of calamities, from partial blindness, vascular dementia, self-harm episodes, various strokes, and breathing problems. Hopkin is upfront on her own exasperation at this terrifying period, at the frustration at the depth and time of the pain suffered and her own role as beleaguered nurse (he would receive round-the-clock care in a nursing home in his last three years), watching her husband deteriorate over a decade and a half. As a statement of independence as a writer, free to come into her own while penning a tribute to the curious genius who nurtured her fiction-writing chops, this is a superb memoir, a snapshot of the Irish illuminati (count the famous cameos) at the fag end of literature's cultural status, an unsentimental peep at one verbivoracious man committed to the world within the word, free from fawning (Hopkin was never fond of his fiction, preferring the memoirs) and steeped in the lush landscape of rural Eire. An essential read for Irish lit enthusiasts from here to Malin Head.

Big Bad
Whitney Collins
Sarabande, 2021

This first volume of stories by Whitney Collins announces the arrival of a major talent. It's an honest-to-goodness event, and not in the sense of that Toyota Sales Event we keep hearing about every few minutes. The thirteen tales collected here have appeared in some of the best literary journals, several of them garnering significant honors in the process, such as a 2020 Pushcart Prize, while the manuscript itself won the 2019 Mary McCarthy Prize in Short Fiction from Sarabande Books, which to its eternal credit has now published it. The combined effect of these pieces is nothing less than stunning.

All this must be wonderful for Collins, who, as the sensitive soul her lively prose clearly reveals her to be, surely smiles to herself occasionally at how this creative triumph was built upon the delicious, delightful, despairing and even despicable predicaments of her long-suffering characters. You've seen them, in gas stations, fast-food restaurants, outlet malls, storefront churches, community colleges, and perhaps in your own backyard at a family picnic or staring back at you from your bathroom mirror. But you've never really met them, until now, and only Collins can make the introductions, because she's the one who's had these people living rent-free in her head.

Just what a clever, compassionate, insightful head Collins has is evident from the first story—"The Nest," wherein the situation of infant twin boys born way too prematurely haunts their overly imaginative sister Frankie—to the last—"Bjorn," which finds a young woman named Bianca equally obsessed with a cyst in her forehead that may be the remnant of her own unborn (un-Bjorn?) twin. In fact, quite a few of these narratives draw their fascination from primal experiences of pregnancy, birth, marriage, sickness, death, and that old reliable favorite of male and female fiction alike, making babies.

None of it seems trivial or topical or secondhand. Rather it is timeless and personal and always cuts to the heart of what it means to be human. You get the feeling that Collins, a modern single mother herself, would also have known how to look good in an animal skin and how to wield a stone ax with the most capable of her Cro Magnon forebears.

In the title story, a woman called Helen mysteriously and repeatedly gives birth to different versions of herself, a most poignant metaphor in Collins' hands. Despite the pun in the title (as in who's afraid of the . . . ?) the big bads here are not usually villains per se, but the bad and bizarre things that happen to everyone, and the warring impulses that cause us to passionately seek or passionately deny the truth of these things, often at the same time. These vividly realized inner conflicts make for good drama and compelling reading.

I am no expert on her main technique of magical realism (or for that matter, on making babies—mine were adopted), so all I can say about the author's stylistic proclivities is that her long years toiling as a humorist, essayist and reporter have served her well as she dives headfirst into fiction. Most of the time she manages to balance horror and humanity, innocence and a hunger for truth bordering on cruelty, and for my money humor is the secret sauce that enables her to do that. I could share some of the lines that made me laugh out loud in this book, but I would rather you found them for yourself, especially as you are likely to pick different lines. There are certainly plenty to choose from. It's as if Shirley Jackson, Dorothy Parker and Flannery O'Connor all showed up on the same day at the same recombinant DNA laboratory.

Although I am not a psychic, I do play one on TV, and I hereby predict that you will remember your initial encounter with this remarkable collection, and you will find yourself returning to it often, discovering details you missed the first time around.

Colin James

A Vampire's Neologisms

An Effortless Explanation of Consciousness

In a real fight
the hero never wins.
The time between
his lunging swing
and contact lets me
use the theatre facilities,
buy some popcorn and soda
then return to my seat
all before his punch lands.
Even reassure my girlfriend
her father's obsession with
quantum mechanics will pass,
since quadrants are like horses,
they eventually sag in the middle
eclipsing a beginning and end.

The Pluralist's Dry Outer Ear

Discipline is a line of taut bums,
soliloquies for the seated.
Confirmation has arrived.
The cart driver will be waiting
at the train station gate.
It is a short journey to the castle.
You are expected.
Introduce yourself generally.
Delve into the claret.
The youngest daughter
may wake you in your twin bed
as you sheepishly sleep it off.
Her sister can ascendantly add
poeticisms or very similar sounds.

Neologisms of the Afterlife

Thinking the word a French derivative,
I hung out in the hotel's back parking lot
near the sky-cake-ornate water fountain.
A helicopter pad was directly opposite
and then cypress trees swayed nonchalantly.
George Sanders had a voice of buttery
    disapproval,
charming pauses between you and see.
Apologizing for arriving so ostentatiously,
his mistress in the throes of her middle-eastern
    phase
will breakfast very soon on strong Turkish coffee
    and figs.

Throwing Shade on the Bump Nasties

The street slang dignitaries
denied my requests
for a writer's block euphemism.
"Seems more like a sexual innuendo"
was not the reaction I expected.
Sour grapes from the Colchagua region.
Seriousness can be misconstrued,
most often exceptionalism rules.
While trying to describe
those humanitarian mannerisms,
I misidentified your sneakers
as under wraps. The charmingly
egalitarian can refute the proletariat,
bring some prey home still alive
purely for training purposes.

The Search for the Perfect Vagina

I first met Lord Maddox in front
of a tobacconist's in North London,
our pipes glowing in the disappearing light.
We withdrew to a worker's cafe
conversing over mugs of thick tea.
He had just returned from two years
in Borneo, appeared frail and withered.
It was there that he indulged in the
initiation rites of an indigenous tribe,
wary and as rare as peaches in Paloma.
He had brought back a priceless keepsake
and it hung from his neck on a gold chain.
That night I slept the sleep of the innocent
woken only by a grunt of incessant persistence.

Expect an Older Vampire

You might see me coming.
I walk bent over,
talk to myself
& drag my right foot.
I don't necessarily travel well
in the dark anymore,
which is unfortunate since
there is an abundance lately.
My long hair is dyed so blonde
it's almost orange.
I am currently the purveyor
& protector of the winds
that all seem to go right through me.
After an impromptu inspection,
my cape is still magnificent.
Towards the bottom edge
there are some problematic stains
& a continuous dampness
I can't quite account for
without completely disrobing formally
& performing a further inspection at my end.
Millions of bacteria vacation
in these crevasses.
They can't afford an ocean view
so settle for a long stroll
to the only perpetual sand dune
where light still has an esoteric hue.
This year's renters
memorize their cabin numbers
by conscientiously counting hair follicles
like that cave giant Polyphemus,
crave soft skin yet edible with three
meals or so yet to choose.

JOHN OLIVER HODGES

WHITE ROSES

In the light by the water a woman played cello while a child in white did flute. Their notes carried over the pond, interrupted once by a train gliding by on its way to Manhattan. Within the music made by woman and child, women with long black hair came round, hair tossed about by intermittent gusts. The women came amongst the people, passing out white roses.

In one lawn-chair sat a guy. The guy watched people receiving the white roses from the women with long black hair. Everybody got one—little kids, old ladies, and a curly-haired young dude in shorts.

The chair the guy sat in was a good chair—sturdy, of multiple pastel colors with a built-in pillow. The guy was not the kind to buy lawn chairs. He had never bought a lawn chair. He found the lawn chair, along with several others, leaning against a garbage can at Asbury Park Beach the last day of summer the year before, when they were closing the place down for the winter months, before the coronovirus came in to ruin the following season.

Though poor, the guy had no problem with rich people. His older brother was, in fact, what they called filthy rich. The guy in the lawn chair was not chaste, either, or obedient to any religion. His only claim to spirituality, and this was no claim at all, was his fondness for forests. His ex-wife and all of his girlfriends had said that he was like a guru. His current girlfriend, on occasion, accused him of being "entitled," of possessing the qualities of a lousy human being. He did not believe her. Mostly she said nice things, and that he

was like a "monk," her word. Right now he was on the mend after eight rounds of chemotherapy. His hair had grown back. It was shoulder length. It was gray, same it was before the disease came along. The guy's ex-wife had always called his hair, not "gray," but "platinum blond."

The guy had not been personally invited to this gathering where they passed out white roses, even though his girlfriend was on the roster of important people scheduled to speak. His girlfriend had not invited him, nor had anybody else, but he wanted to be here. He hated what was going on. He wanted it to STOP, all capital letters, same as it was written on the poster secured to the lectern. He wanted to help. He wanted to add his number to the force against it. He wanted to be of service.

From his chair, he watched the young women with long black hair hand white roses out. He thought: *will they give me one?* He watched the young dude with curly hair and fancy running sneakers get one. He watched people around him getting their roses. And he wanted a rose. He wiggled in his chair a bit, slightly agitated, as if saying over here, here I am, I'd love to get one too.

The young women with long black hair passed him by, giving white roses to everybody but him. They had armfuls, plenty to spare. Maybe they knew about him. Something told them. They felt it. They knew that he was from Florida, that he'd lived in Mississippi, that he'd heard and repeated certain jokes as a child, that he'd stood around, as an adult, while acquaintances went on about people who worked longer hours for less money, scooping up the work. Back then he was what people called "redneck." His girlfriend, a poet, was one of the speakers tonight, and she too had the long black beautiful hair.

A voice expanded in the air. People clapped. A female professor said some things. A councilwoman said some things, raising her fist as a new train pounded by. Two youngsters from the high school, a boy and girl, took the mic. The girl said some things. And then the boy read his essay about how messed up things became when the coronavirus hit, and so many of his privileges were stripped away. People saw him different now. He was not what he had been, when he could walk into the Starbucks of a summer's day, sweating, with no shirt on. He said that the support coming in from the larger community and throughout the neighborhoods was appreciated, but much of it, he knew, was for show, done out of political necessity. This is the world we live in. He finished his essay to strong, heartfelt applause, and the guy in the lawn chair thought: *this could be the future president.*

The mayor stepped up to the lectern. The mayor resembled Senator Cory Booker from nearby Newark, not because he was bald. A similar rhythm and ethos came out in his words. After his speech, the mayor mentioned that his childhood friend flew in from Chicago to be here tonight. The friend went up to the lectern and the two of them embraced. Another train passed along the tracks perpendicular to the duck pond. Another woman with long black hair streaming down her back sang opera, forehead crinkled with emotion, with yearning, with a sadness dedicated to the women whose faces were displayed on the poster attached to the lectern—those women.

The guy's girlfriend, the poet, was introduced by a woman who looked very proud to be introducing her. The woman looked

smitten as she read out his girlfriend's accomplishments, the magazines she had published in, and the awards she had won. At the end of her introduction, the introducer didn't want to move away from the lectern. She wanted to stay there, in solidarity, so in solidarity she stood. As his girlfriend read a poem, looking fierce and limitless, the woman who'd introduced her beamed, all this admiration. I love my girlfriend, the guy thought. After the poem, his girlfriend said some words about women warriors.

Next came a Protestant preacher from the area whose dilemma before taking stage, the guy imagined, was *Do I or do I not mention Jesus? If I mention Jesus, I'll be putting my thing on others. If I don't mention Jesus, I'll be betraying my Lord.* Maybe he mentioned Jesus. Maybe he did not. The guy in the lawn chair that he found against a garbage can at Asbury Beach stopped paying close attention, as he still was thinking about how awesome his girlfriend was, and anyway he'd tried Jesus. He'd given believing in Jesus a decent shot but it didn't work out. Jesus, in the end, was useless during his cancer woes.

It was dark now. It was dark, and the final woman at the lectern, a woman with long black hair, said, "We gave to everybody here white roses. We passed them out to you at the beginning. The roses represent our commitment. The white roses are a symbol, a token a statement that we are going to try harder to release this hatred, to make a renewed commitment to fight."

The guy, from his lawn chair, looked around. He'd not been invited, but had come.

"Let us now release our white roses into the pond," the beautiful woman with long ack hair said, and the guy watched the eople there gathered, the mixed families nd old ladies and the young dude with rly hair and fancy running sneakers— ey all stepped down to the water of the ck pond, surrounding the pond as if to nbrace it as a community. They released eir roses into the water, pushing them t like paper boats.

The guy then watched from his chair as e people, many shivering from the cold at had set in deep as the night began, rried away from the water, moving away om the pond in the direction of the street here their cars and utility vehicles were arked. The guy remained in his chair, eyes xed on the pond whose roses shimmered the moonlight, a small galaxy of flower- g matter. He watched as a cloud cut below e moon, and the twinkling stars dimmed.

REVIEW | Paul John Adams

Windows into Mike Kleine's Universe

Burnin' Oceans
Mike Kleine
Surfaces, 2020

Where the Sky Meets the Ocean and the Air Tastes Like Metal and The Birds Don't Make a Sound
Mike Kleine and Dan Hoy
Trnsfr Books, July 2021

Mike Kleine's *Burnin' Oceans* is a short work—pamphlet length— that can be reread easily, multi- le times. Here, I will attempt to interro-

gate the work. In the process, I will offer a review containing more words than the text under analysis. I invite others to write even longer analyses of my analysis. Note that this critique is all spoiler, all night long.

If *Burnin' Oceans* is telling a story, what story does it tell?

There is an unnamed protagonist who speaks, at times, in the first person, as "i," and who is implied in "we." "i" starts the story and "i" ends the story, within a frame of "instrumentals"—music such as would begin and end a television program. This "i" is never really an agent in the story. "i" does not do anything consequential—"i" only takes self-contained, inconsequential actions such as punching rocks to express frustration. Otherwise, "i" only has things happen to him or her. "i" exists in a dan- gerous environment, one that has possibly been ruined by humanity, possibly ruined by some natural malevolence, possibly cursed be daemons and black magic, and most probably it is a little bit of all of the above.

There are several named characters in the text. All are part of the peer group or "gang" of "i", and all have commercialism built into their names; all have alliterating names, and their surnames are brands of luxury cars.

The named characters have various things happen to them and do various things. I believe it is fair to say they don't have full agency. It is less honest to say that they are characters than that they are ele- ments of the environment of "i". Some die, some party, some attempt and some suc- ceed at suicide. They may be capable of casting magic spells that permanently change "everything," but basically they are part of a chaotic, disjointed, both post-apocalyptic and pre-civilized timeless disaster-world. The universe itself is infinite, warped, unsympathetic, and permeated by blue rays of despair. The sky is subject to fragmenting.

There is one apparent attempt at communication—a failed attempt—between "i" and a character named thomas tesla via phone text-messages. "i" appears to bungle the communication, as "i" is distracted by some personal reflections while thomas appears to be trying to communicate a more pragmatic message or warning. The exchange is terminated abruptly.

The characters who are not named are of more potential significance than the named characters. They are largely absent from the story, except that they exist on a sort of different plane from "i". They are the father of "i", killed by a tree (hanged? or quite literally killed by the tree?), and an unidentified "she", who could be the mother or lover of "i", or could bear some other unknown relationship to "i". "she" is presented to us as in a kind of permanent state of suspense before an anticipated execution.

It is conceivable that "i" is an orphan whose parents were killed in an earlier time or it is possible that "i" is only fatherless, whereas the death of "she" remains indeterminate. "i" may be despairing of reaching "she" before the moment of death.

The story ends with "i" alone, separated from the peer group, in a bleak, arid, toxic world, both primitive and futuristic, still timeless. "i" is in a separate, permanent state of pre-death suspense, apparently about to be killed by the hostile force of the sun, but it is not certain that the death blow falls before the closing instrumentals.

WHAT IS HAPPENING WITH THE LANGUAGE IN THIS WORK?

Kleine's characters tend to be limited in their ability to emote. They engage in occasional speech events or outbursts, but they do not typically speak at length. They do not engage in the kind of dialog that humans typically engage in. Rather "dialog" takes more the form of individual lines that don't properly engage with the speech of the other. Comments may be tangential, may only partially communicate, may miss their marks, and may sometimes be apropos by accident. Comments often resemble the kind of communication that takes place in online forums where speech may be ironic, may be pithy, may lack context, but in one way or another the communication is incomplete, unsatisfactory, and does not render itself fully comprehensible. This form of communication suggests the author is protesting the limitations of language for true communication, and he is perhaps highlighting the isolation and alienation that result. In Mike Kleine's world, due to a kind of language failure, whether physically isolated or together people inevitably find themselves facing a hostile world alone.

WHAT IS DANGER?

In this work, danger is most often chaotic and impersonal. In the Mike Kleine universe, even "personal" violence in which someone is intentionally targeted has such an unpredictable and arbitrary nature as to ppear anarchic and thus "impersonal." ad things happen. Whether there is an gent or not, the agent cannot be reasoned ith, understood, or deterred. Whether uman or inhuman, natural, supernatural, r unnatural, everything is an element of nvironmental danger.

Wнat does this нave to do wiтн *Twin Peaks?*

robably not much, though some initial eed of inspiration may have arisen from om the show (and there are indications of nany other tangential influences such as itano's *Sonatine* and several musical orks.) Perhaps worth a note, the first im- ge in episode eight of the first season of *win Peaks*, following the instrumental pening credit sequence, is of the sun shin- ıg through palm trees, while *Burnin' Oceans* egins with burning palm trees and a first limpse of the hostile sun which seems bout to destroy the protagonist in the end. *urnin' Oceans* starts with time code refer- nce to *Twin Peaks* "part 8".

Wнat furтнеr notes need to ве made?

lthough there is a pervading anticipation f doom, it seems humanity and culture an never be eradicated. If poetry can *nearly* e effaced, it still leaves traces (in the form f "smudge poetry" in the sand, and an o.g. poem" carved in rocks.) Hedonistic leasure and temporary escape can be had hen blending in with the crowd—skinny ipping and vogueing parties beckon—lost ands can be miraculously restored—some ıcky bastard may find himself "immune"

to acid rains that threaten others. And there is escape into cyclical reviewing of entertainment media.

Sum iт up; Wнaт's tнis aвouт?

This can be about many things, and it doesn't open up all its secrets to the reader, but I may have found one window into un- derstanding a few aspects of the work. *Burnin' Oceans* can be a (qualified) celebra- tion of the relative safety and ephemeral happiness that is enjoyed through appreci- ation of the arts and connections with close friends and acquaintances, and at the same time it can be a cry of protest that these things are inadequate, that the larger world remains hostile, that we tend to iso- late, that language ultimately fails to pro- vide a satisfactory connection with others, that art and friends are fated to dissolve away and leave one stranded. It may also be an expression of a personal loss of a father, or of family members, as well as expressing the feelings of a relationship failure, as the "i" and the "she" are doomed to separate extinctions.

I draw all my conclusions tentatively, as it seems fitting for me to do. Thus is *Burnin' Oceans.*

The novel *Where the Sky Meets the Ocean and the Air Tastes Like Metal and the Birds Don't Make a Sound* is longer than *Burnin' Oceans*, and therefore I will deal with it more briefly. It is coauthored by Mike Kleine and Dan Hoy, and it appears that in Hoy, Kleine has met a kindred literary spirit.

I have seen the development of Kleine's universe through five prior novels now and several shorter works between, each of which has its own unique charms. His books find ways to intersect with one another through commonalities of style, recurrent characters, and shared thematic obsessions. Now, Kleine and Hoy's new work forms another link in the chain. What makes this one distinct from Kleine's solo works is that, on a superficial level, it adopts a more conventional narrative thrust. It takes the form of a buddy adventure driven by a central conflict.

The two main protagonists—Michael and Daniel—are agents in ways that the characters of *Burnin' Oceans* are not. They have agency in their own story, and literally they are *investigating agents* seeking to "solve" a murder mystery.

Now, the very premise of trying to solve a mystery through logical deduction in a world where events are not linked by clear cause and effect, where there is no dividing line between the natural and the supernatural, and where powerful, rich, and hedonistic entities carry out various obscure plots from somewhere in the shadows, is fundamentally absurd—which is why Michael and Daniel mainly do their investigating through a combination of brutal interrogations (alienating us from them as humans) and legwork, following leads from one strange character and one exotic locale to the next. This formula, and the tension between established expectations and the novel's refusal to fulfill them, undermine the conventionality of the plot and reveal its function as a mystery-laced parody on the level of story and a playful literary experiment on the level of style.

If there is a cinematic analogy to this book (as there often is in a Kleine project, with or without coauthors) it is as if two Lemmy Cautions had dropped out throug a crack in Godard's *Alphaville*, and then the found themselves in a world of Darq Mag icks, centaur men, melting skies, and cult like organizations such as the Architects c Q'Noor.

In between the casting of spells, the at tending of parties, the encounters with mortal danger, the inventorying of items o clothes, and the making of many life an death decisions ("*but mostly death*," think Michael), we stumble upon one of the mos entertaining chapters, a listing chapte that identifies all the conversation topic between two characters that we presum were discussed in a few hours, though i should have taken years to treat them al with any depth. This chapter should tickl the fancy of fans of the time-honored list ing tradition that spans both pre-moder and post-modern fiction. And if you're practitioner of bibliomancy, you may wan to use this chapter to random-select th next conversation you have with you friends (try "mirror neurons," for in stance).

And then comes the final culmination, deadly clash with ancient and mysteriou forces, and if you think I'll spoil the plo now, sorry, I forgot to tell you that switched off spoiler mode several para graphs ago, but don't you fear. Whateve doom may come to our protagonists o their nemeses, the Mike-Kleine-and-Dan Hoy universe will persist in all direction and all dimensions, perhaps damaged perhaps forever changed, but never able t be snuffed out. And whatever remain churning in it's darq, mysterious heart, w can be sure this universe will regenerat new terrors and new joys in whatever tex these gentlemen cook up next.

A. Salcedo
translated from the Spanish by
Daniel Beauregard

V

from *The Hydrogen Mafia*

Not everything that shines
is light
Too the brilliance of dogs
is heavy
Their mix of hair
made entirely of free cells
brings the rising of the night

Not everything that screams
is dust
There's also the plants, with their
old laws, that create worlds
of concepts ridiculous and inevitable
This is the leaf, it's my limit
This is the stem, it's the bridge
These are the roots,
thanks to them I'm rooted

Not everything that dances
is fun
There is also muscular death
and death by desiccation
and the men of the port
who wear beards upon pale skin

Not everything that loves
really loves
Sometimes one fools themselves
for the heat
for the fear of the sick
but if you'd like
we can bet a kiss

Not everything I touch
is ass
I also visit hospitals
and go up in the elevators randomly
I also wake up early
after having dreamed
of something, what was it, well something,
and drink coffee while staring at the cup

Not everything that exists
has a name
There are also bugs that
laugh at time
and men and women
that cry when they watch movies
There are also ways to live
that are still uncoded
The system doesn't support them
but the system is large
and there's always room for contraband

Not everything that looks
is an eye
Electrons also look
They stop to observe the grand castle
periodically
And the grass also looks
after many years
continues to feed
the chain of tissues and passions

Not everything that shines
is light
The shadow too illuminates
its secret is safe
and it's thin the infinite line
that divides my hand
from eternity

CHRIS SUMBERG

WEDNESDAY MORNING, RAIN

BRANCH OUT, LIVE a LITTLE

Keep doing X until it fucking kills you—which it will. Keeping on doing X is no longer about X, as in your rare honest hours, you might agree. Doing X is now about having done X for so fucking long that to abandon X would mean to abandon your entire adult life to this point. X is about the only fucking investment you have ever made. Until that day when the universe collapses—any day now—X is all you have, so you think, to hold near. It's nuts, obviously. Fucking around with X to the degree you fuck around with X is unnatural, but, so they say, being unnaturally focused on X is "what it takes," though, if honest, which you're certainly not, you despise almost 100 percent of those they-sayers. Kills the remaining bits, the A through W and Y through Z, this over-focus on X does. You should know that better than anyone who ever did X. Which will it be, which path is the correct one? It's said that X marks the spot, for treasure, in stories, but this is not a story, and X might just be marking some sort of grave, and it could be yours, pal. Will yourself, then, to at least consider if not A through W, at least, Y.

Sadly, It's Down to You

You can always and forever find reason for not doing things. Canceling tha once-jolly, now-grim, mark on the ever-fore shortening calendar, a shadow moving visibl across relentless lines of weeks and too-soo days. Always ducking away. And, just notin no one, least of all you, believes your feebl stories as you duck. Forevermore, then, yo continue sitting, an uncarved Easter Islan block, lump-like in the rain, the water pou ing down your unformed face like tear which is to say a lump of cold, wet stone en trenched on a bluff above a perfectly walka ble shore. Finding yourself alone with you non-thoughts and daydream ambitions, yo simply repeat those thoughts and daydream muscle memory in service to flab. Reason can be generated, of course; this is a turbu lent world that crushes dreams like bee cans, and especially daydreams (like sod cans). Forgoing all real-world, forward mo mentum, though, seems a bit extreme, sa and frightened. Not that this is your *essence* no, it's an understandable bulwark agains certain-seeming failure. Doing something i likely, the cure, but there are so many some things and only one unlucky one, which i you. Things, then, things, so many, yes, to many damned things, will sit unmovable un til someone, maybe, sadly, you, or mayb some random self- and life-detesting dicta tor—or if you're lucky, some selfless soul (bu don't hold your breath on that one, you)—un til they or you can, at least some of the time or occasionally, find some reason in doin things.

Contributors

[Pa]ul John Adams is the author of *To Fail With Flying Col-[or]s*, a novel of psychiatric quackery. He currently re-[si]des with his wife and kids in Glen Allen, Virginia, [U]SA. Paul can occasionally be spotted gambling it up in [th]e "Big-O" game at the Maryland Live! Casino.

[W]ill Alexander is a poet, novelist, essayist, aphorist, [pl]aywright, philosopher, visual artist, and pianist. He is [a] recipient of a California Arts Council Fellowship, a [PE]N/Oakland Josephine Miles Award, and a Whiting [Fe]llowship, among many others. He has taught at sev-[er]al universities, including the Jack Kerouac School of [Di]sembodied Poetics and the University of California–[Sa]n Diego. He lives in California.

[D]aniel Beauregard recently published two poetry [ch]apbooks, *Total Darkness Means No Notifications* [(Co]nstruther Press, 2021) and *Anatomizing Uncanny Alley* [(S]elf Fuck, 2021), and is the co-founder of OOMPH! [Pr]ess. He lives in Buenos Aires.

[Je]si Buell is an artist from Upstate New York. Under the [n]ame Jesi Bender, she helms KERNPUNKT Press, a home [fo]r experimental writing. She is the author of *Kinderkranken-[ha]us* (Sagging Meniscus, 2021) and *The Book of the Last Word* [(W]hiskey Tit, 2019). Her shorter writing has appeared in [Th]e Rumpus, *Split Lip, Adroit Journal*, and others.

[Ke]vin Boniface, an artist, writer and postman in Hud-[de]rsfield, West Yorkshire, UK, is the author of *Round [Ab]out Town* (Uniformbooks, 2018) and *Lost in the Post* [(O]ld Street Publishing, 2008).

[Er]asmilus blogs at discontinuednotes.com.

[M]arvin Cohen is the author of many novels, plays, and [co]llections of essays, stories, and poems. He lives on the [Lo]wer East Side of Manhattan.

[B]rian Evenson's latest book is *The Glassy, Burning Floor of [He]ll* (Coffee House Press, Aug. 2021).

[C]olin Gee is founder and editor of *The Gorko Gazette*, a [d]aily and quarterly zine that publishes headlines, re-[vi]ews, cartoons, and bad poetry. He is director of the [la]nguage department at the Universidad de la Sierra [Ju]árez in Oaxaca, México.

[Ja]ke Goldsmith, 24, is a writer with cystic fibrosis and [th]e founder of The Barbellion Prize, a book prize for ill [an]d disabled authors. He is the author of a memoir, [N]either Weak Nor Obtuse (SM, 2022).

Tyler C. Gore has been cited three times as a Notable Essayist by *Best American Essays*. His essay collection, *My Life in Crime*, will be published in Sept. 2022 by SM.

Genese Grill is a German scholar, essayist, and transla-tor living in Plainfield, Vermont. She is the author of a scholarly study, *The World as Metaphor in Robert Musil's "The Man without Qualities": Possibility as Reality* (Camden House, 2012), and the translator of a collection of Robert Musil's short prose, *Thought Flights* (Contra Mundum, 2015), a book of his short stories, *Unions* (Contra Mundum, 2019), and another of his plays and writings on theater, *Theater Symptoms: Plays and Writings on Drama* (Contra Mundum, 2020).

John Patrick Higgins is a playwright, short story writer, screenwriter and director. He lives in Belfast.

John Oliver Hodges has work in *Hash, Juked, Bull, Swink, Frigg*, and *Crag*. He has work in two-syllable journals as well: *Hobart, Gravel, Gone Lawn* and *Treehouse*. He is the au-thor of three books: *Quizzleboon, The Love Box*, and *War of the Crazies*. He lives in New Jersey where he teaches creative writing, via Zoom, for the Gotham Writers' Workshop.

Colin James, author of *Resisting Probability* (SM, 2017), was born in the north of England near Chester. He spent most of his youth in Massachusetts before mov-ing back to England and working as a Postman for The Royal Mail, then as a Trackman for British Rail. He met his American wife, Jane, in Chester and they currently reside in Western Massachusetts. He is a great admirer of the Scottish landscape painter, John Mackenzie.

Paul Kavanagh wrote *Kitchen Sink* (Aiurea Press).

Kurt Luchs is the author of *Falling in the Direction of Up* (SM, 2020), *One of These Things Is Not Like the Other* (Finish-ing Line Press, 2019), and the humor collection *It's Funny Until Someone Loses an Eye (Then It's Really Funny)* (SM, 2017). He lives in Michigan.

Linda Mannheim is the author of three books of fic-tion: *This Way to Departures* (shortlisted for the Edge Hill Prize), *Above Sugar Hill*, and *Risk*. She's had work in *The Nation, Granta*, and *3:AM Magazine*. Originally from New York, she lives in London.

Andrew McKeown teaches English at the University of Poitiers. Under the name Stan McEwan, he is the au-thor of the poetry collection *You What?*

R.S. Mengert completed an MFA in poetry at Syracuse University. His work has appeared in *Pensive, SurVision, Zymbol, Poor Yorick, Maintenant, Poetry is Dead, ABZ, Four Chambers, The Café Review, Fjords, San Pedro River Review,* and *Enizagam.* He lives in Tempe, AZ, with his wife and an unusually loud cat.

Stephen Moles, founder of the Dark Meaning Research Institute, regularly carries out undercover literary assignments aimed at bringing about the linguistic singularity for the benefit of society. His latest book is *Your Dark Meaning, Mouse* (SM, Nov. 2021).

Robert Musil (1880–1942) is the author of *Young Törless* and *The Man Without Qualities*.

M.J. Nicholls is the author of the novels *Trimming England* (SM, 2021), *Scotland Before the Bomb* (SM, 2019), The *1002nd Book to Read Before You Die* (SM, 2018), *The Quiddity of Delusion* (SM, 2017), *The House of Writers* (SM, 2016), and *A Postmodern Belch* (2014). He lives in Glasgow.

Kathleen Nicholls is an author and illustrator, best known for *Go Your Crohn Way,* the first of three books loosely based on her own experiences with chronic illness. She lives and works in central Scotland.

Doug Nufer is the author of many novels and poetry collections, including *Rotalever Revelator* (SM, 2020), *Metamorphosis* (SM, 2018), *The Me Theme* (SM, 2017), *Lifeline Rule* (Spuyten Duyvil, 2015), *Lounge Acts* (Insert Blanc, 2013), *The Dammed* (ubu.com, 2011), *By Kelman Out of Pessoa* (Les Figues, 2011), *We Were Werewolves* (Make Now, 2008), *The Mud at Man/The River Boys* (soultheft records, 2006), *On the Roast* (Chiasmus, 2004), *Negativeland* (Autonomedia, 2004), and *Never Again* (Black Square, 2004). He sells wine in Seattle.

Maureen Owen is the author of eleven books of poetry, including *Edges of Water* (Chax, 2013).

Sarah Pazur is a Michigan-based writer with a PhD in Educational Leadership. Her work has appeared or is forthcoming in *Pithead Chapel, JMWW, Hybrid Pedagogy, Phi Delta Kappan* and other publications.

LJ Pemberton is a writer/artist living in Los Angeles, California. Her essays, poetry, and award-winning stories have been featured in *The Los Angeles Review, PANK, LEVEE, Hobart, Drunk Monkeys, VICE, The Brooklyn Rail,* and elsewhere. New work is forthcoming from *Cosmonauts Avenue* and *The Northwest Review*. She currently reviews fiction for *Publishers Weekly*. Her (yet unpublished) novel, *STARBOI,* is a queer tale of obsession and heartbreak set in the recent past. She is the editor of the *Bureau of Complaint*.

Ben Pester writes fiction and lives in London. His collection of stories *Am I in the Right Place?* was published in May 2021 by Boiler House Press in the UK. His work ha[s] appeared in *Granta, Five Dials, Hotel* and more.

A. Salcedo is a pseudonym for an anonymous contem[po]rary poet residing in Buenos Aires, Argentina. The[ir] first book, *La Mafia del Hidrogeno* (Nulú Bonsai, 2013) [is] currently in its third printing and the sequel to it, *El Ár[bol Liquido,* is forthcoming from Nulú Bonsai.

Jesse Salvo's short fiction has been featured in *Hoba[rt,] Barren Magazine, Menacing Hedge, Pacifica Review, X-Ray L[it,] Cowboy Jamboree, Tiny Molecules,* and *BULL*. Before that, h[e] spent three years working for online comedy magazine[s] which were not *Foreign Affairs* but did produce the tang[i]ble benefit of keeping the heat in his apartment on.

Mike Silverton's poetry appeared in the late 60s and ear[ly] 70s in *Harper's, The Nation, Wormwood Review, Poetry Now some/thing, Chelsea, Prairie Schooner, Elephant* and elsewher[e.] William Cole included Mike's poems in four anthologie[s:] *Eight Lines and Under* (Macmillan, 1967), *Pith and Vinegar* (S[i]mon and Schuster, 1969), *Poetry Brief* (Macmillan, 1971[)] and *Poems One Line & Longer* (Grossman, 1973). His collec[]tion *Anvil on a Shoestring* is forthcoming from SM.

Julian Stannard's most recent collection is *Heat Wa[ve]* (Salt, 2020).

Chris Sumberg has recent publications in *AHO[Y] Comics' Happy Hour, 251 (American Bystander), Stanchio[n]* and *Portland Monthly Magazine*.

Matthew Tomkinson is a writer, composer, and doctor[al] candidate in Theatre Studies at the University of Britis[h] Columbia. His chapbook *For a Long Time* is out with Fro[g] Hollow Press, and his debut collection of experiment[al] short fiction, *Archaic Torso of Gumby,* coauthored with Geo[f]frey Morrison, is available at Gordon Hill Press.

Thomas Walton is the author of four books: *Good Morn[]ing Bonecrusher!* (upcoming, Spuyten Duyvil), *All the Use[]less Things Are Mine* (SM, 2020), *The World Is All That Does Be[]fall Us* (Ravenna Press, 2019), and, with Elizabeth Coop[]erman, *The Last Mosaic* (SM, 2018). He lives in Seattle.

David Winner's third novel, *Enemy Combatant* (Marc[h] 2021), received a Kirkus-starred review and was a Pub[]lisher's Weekly/Booklife Editor's Pick. He is the co-editor o[f] *Writing the Virus,* a New York Times briefly-noted Antholog[y.] His Kirkus-recommended second novel, *Tyler's Last,* cam[e] out in 2015, while his first, *The Cannibal of Guadalajara,* wo[n] the 2009 Gival Press Novel Award and was nominated fo[r] the National Book Award. His work has appeared in *The Vi[l]lage Voice, Fiction, The Iowa Review, The Millions* and *The Kenyo[n] Review*. He is a senior editor at *Statorec* magazine and a reg[]ular contributor to *The Brooklyn Rail*.

Lightning Source UK Ltd.
Milton Keynes UK
UKHW050755241221
396187UK00006B/416